# Rebirth

ALSO BY KAMAL RAVIKANT

*Love Yourself Like Your Life Depends on It*

*Live Your Truth*

# *Rebirth*

A Fable of Love, Forgiveness,
and Following Your Heart

## KAMAL RAVIKANT

NEW YORK BOSTON

Copyright © 2017 by Kamal Ravikant
Maps by Jeffrey L. Ward

Jacket design by Alison Forner
Jacket copyright © 2017 by Hachette Book Group, Inc.

Hachette Books
Hachette Book Group
1290 Avenue of the Americas
New York, NY 10104
hachettebookgroup.com
twitter.com/hachettebooks

First edition: January 2017

Hachette Books is a division of Hachette Book Group, Inc.

The Hachette Books name and logo are trademarks of Hachette Book Group, Inc.

The publisher is not responsible for websites (or their content) that are not owned by the publisher.

The Hachette Speakers Bureau provides a wide range of authors for speaking events. To find out more, go to www.hachettespeakersbureau.com or call (866) 376-6591.

Library of Congress Cataloging-in-Publication Data

Names: Ravikant, Kamal author.
Title: Rebirth : a fable / Kamal Ravikant.
Description: First edition. | New York : Hachette Books, 2017.
Identifiers: LCCN 2016037257| ISBN 9780316312288 (hardback) | ISBN 9781478940616 (audio cd) | ISBN 9781478940623 (audio download)
Subjects: LCSH: Spiritual life—Fiction. | Christian pilgrims and pilgrimages—Fiction. | Camino de Santiago de Compostela—Fiction. | BISAC: FICTION / Visionary & Metaphysical. | FICTION / Family Life.
Classification: LCC PS3618.A9375 R43 2017 | DDC 813/.6—dc23 LC record available at https://lccn.loc.gov/2016037257

ISBNs: 978-0-316-31228-8 (hardcover), 978-0-316-31225-7 (ebook)

Printed in the United States of America

LSC-C

10 9 8 7 6 5 4 3 2 1

*To my mother. To Trish. To Robin. To Cheryl. To Kristine.*
*Amazing women, all.*

# Author's Note

Although a work of fiction, *Rebirth* is based on my experience of the Camino de Santiago. The Camino is timeless. Regardless of which century you walk it, the core experience remains unchanged. Therefore, I've kept any mention of current technology to a minimum.

I wish you all the magic this journey gave me.

—Kamal

## The Secret to Flight

Don't flap your wings so hard. It only
exhausts you.

Close your eyes. Lean into the currents,
say *yes*. Let the wind raise you higher and
higher. So easy. That's what Eagles do.

Oh, this is the secret to life as well.

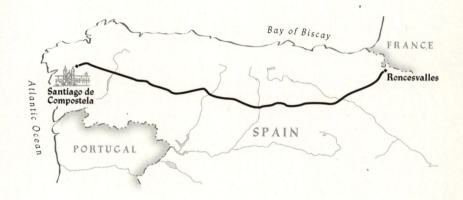

# Rebirth

# Prologue

At the banks of the Ganges, I perform a ritual as old as this land and as foreign to me as the river rushing by. A priest hands me the box, then places his palms together. I open it. Inside, gritty dust resembling crushed charcoal. I hold the box out and empty it. My father's ashes spiral through the air and land softly in the water below. The river claims them with the sureness of an old lover who waits, patiently.

A lone tree with thick, leafy branches leans over me. After the priest leaves, I sit down, press my back against the trunk. The branches sway slightly, the evening grows cooler, the red in the sky deepens, and the river flows closer. Water laps against my feet. Somewhere on the other shore a bell rings.

Behind me, steps lead to a temple with a domed roof. Children stand outside, selling garlands made from orange marigolds. Men in white dhotis walk by, talking loudly, laughing. The moon, now high above, is the size of a small coin.

My neck is stiff. I haven't eaten all day but don't feel any hunger. There is an aching numbness in the back of my eyes.

I walk to the rented car. The driver, waiting for me on the steps, flicks a glowing cigarette into the river and walks alongside. A monkey scurries past and jumps onto a brick wall outside the temple. It screeches loudly as children surround me. They reach at my pockets, grab my arms, tug my sleeves. In the crowd are old women holding out cupped hands.

"It is tradition," the driver says to me. "You must give money to the elderly, the poor."

I barely hear him over the children. Hands brush my palms and take the rupees and paise. I walk faster but they hold on to me, grab my legs, my waist.

"No," the driver says, pushing the children away. "The elderly, give it to them."

To my left, at the edge of the temple, old women sit in a line. I drop money in empty bowls before them, moving down the row. One woman is missing a leg. Her stump sticks out from under her sari. Another is blind and holds her bowl out when she hears me coming. She stares ahead with irises the color of milk. When the coins drop in her bowl, she moves it side to side, making them jingle. The woman next to her lifts her bowl toward me. My pockets are empty.

"I'm sorry," I say, but we don't speak the same language.

She tilts her head and opens her mouth. Her face is cross-hatched with wrinkles and her hands are withered. She shakes the bowl.

"I'm so sorry."

She lowers the bowl and looks down. The children grab at my pockets. The driver pulls them away.

In a hotel room, away from crowds and funeral pyres, I spread open a map of India, trace the contours with my fingers. Deserts, rivers, valleys, lakes, mountains. I rub my eyes with the heel of my palm until the map blurs.

My aunt was the one who told me about his diagnosis. I

stared at black-and-white tiles on the kitchen floor, half-eaten tuna sandwich in one hand, said "uh-huh" into the phone, listened to her talk, and all that time, swallowed hard to keep memories from rushing up my stomach into my throat. "He is your father," she said. "What happened does not matter. You must take care of him."

Through shuttered windows, auto-rickshaws and cars honk. With a blink the map comes into focus. Colors separate. Lines snap back and form borders, roads, rivers. I finished what I came here to do. What now? I'm not ready to return home. Coming to the country of my father's birth has shaken something inside.

The air is humid and smells of *raat ki rani*, night queen, a small, white flower. The ceiling fan creaks. I remember George Mallory, my favorite childhood hero. When asked why he climbed Everest, he replied, "Because it's there." It was the truest answer a ten-year-old boy had ever read. Same for a twenty-seven-year-old. Perhaps even more so.

What to do next? Keep moving. Leave behind the past, the fears, the guilt, and lose myself in the new. With movement, there's action. And with action, perhaps there are answers.

For the next two months, I wander north. In train compartments with families who eat out of round tins, the smell of *pharantas* filling the air, they gesture and invite me to share their food. Through streets past oxen with droopy eyes, camels pulling wooden carts, and women wearing bright-colored saris, garlands of white flowers in their hair, driving motorcycles. In ancient buses as they labor up winding roads, the drivers reaching out to wipe mist off the windshield with bare hands.

I find myself in Dharamsala, a small cloud-covered village at the edge of the Himalayas. The Dalai Lama's monastery is here. Each morning, I hike from my guesthouse to sit in the main sanctuary, and listen to the throaty chants of the orange-robed monks until my legs fall asleep.

One dawn, I step outside to take a break and stretch. An old monk turns the prayer wheels recessed into the walls. It takes him a long while to turn them all. He repeats this process several times.

What must it take to be a monk, to give up life and love and family, to focus only on the inner self? The next time he nears me, I bow. He bows in return and holds one hand up in a blessing. The other holds a string of large, wooden beads.

"I have a question."

"It's okay," he says, his voice a whisper.

"How do you find peace?"

He is solemn for a moment, then smiles the biggest, warmest smile. Behind him, far in the distance, are sharp-edged mountains. I feel like they must when sunlight envelops them after a cold, winter night.

"Simple," he says slowly. "Simple question."

I grin. "Not for me."

"Where are you from?"

"America."

He nods thoughtfully, as if that explains everything.

"I say 'yes,'" he says. "To all that happens, I say 'yes.'"

He bows and returns to his prayer wheels. Snow plumes drift lazily across mountain peaks, the rising sun coloring them a golden yellow.

Back in the guesthouse, I tell an Italian tourist about my

wanderings over the last few months. Unlike other backpack-ers, I haven't joined any ashrams or partied at raves in Goa. Not even taken one yoga class. Heck, I wouldn't know how to meditate if my life depended on it. My first time traveling abroad, less than five thousand dollars to my name, and my job's gone. Yet, I cannot stop.

"I understand," he says.

Fresh out of college, he's already racked up over a dozen countries. He tells me about the places he wants to visit, but his dream is to hike a pilgrimage in Spain called the Camino de Santiago. His grandfather did it, his father did it, and one day, before he marries, he and his bride-to-be will do it together.

"Everyone finds themselves on the Camino," he says. "Everyone."

Just about the exact opposite of my travels so far.

"How long does it take?" I ask.

"Seven days, maybe," he says. Easy enough.

I head south and think about it more and more. Spain. The land of Don Quixote. Of wine. Paella and flamenco. So differ-ent than here. Perhaps better as it has zero claim on my history, nothing to jog memories. By the time I reach my aunt's house in New Delhi, Spain is more on my mind than not.

It's April and already the heat is unbearable. I spend the days in the garden poring over her husband's collection of anthropology textbooks. That and avoiding my aunt's ques-tions. Nights are spent listening to the watchman walk the streets, blowing his whistle, knocking his bamboo cane on the ground. It's time to pull the trigger.

"What are you going to do?" my aunt asks one morning over breakfast.

Once she was someone I knew through photographs and phone calls. Now I'm in her house, eating chapatis and *daal*.

Then, to her husband, something she's repeated daily like a mantra.

"The boy's flight left when he was wandering around."

She reaches over, runs her hand through my hair. It's grown messy, time to return to a high and tight. I miss that clean buzz-cut feeling.

"When are you getting married, *beta*?"

If you're single, in your late twenties, and visiting India, you'll get asked that question by everyone you meet. And if you're family, it never ends.

"You shouldn't be alone," she says. "You need a woman to take care of you."

"I'm okay. I can take care of myself."

"It's just a stage, *beta*, you will grow out of it."

Her husband glances up from his newspaper. "I will put a marriage ad in the paper for you."

"Marriage ad?"

"You will get so many responses, a good boy like you from America."

Meaning people will see a walking, talking green card.

"And a doctor too," he says.

"I'm not a doctor. I'm just thinking about going to med school."

"Nothing to worry about." He nods. "Doctor sounds good."

Now I'm a green card with dollar signs.

"What a wedding." My aunt rubs her hands together, bangles clinking. "We will buy beautiful saris for your wife, we will dance in your *bharat*."

"I'm going home," I say.

Silence.

"With a stopover in Europe," I add.

"*Arre*, Amit, what is the rush? Just wait and see the responses you will get."

"I'll check out a pilgrimage in Spain."

A long pause. Her husband coughs.

"Pilgrimage?"

"You should stay in India," my aunt says. "We have more pilgrimages than people."

"I already booked my ticket."

She waves at her husband. "Speak some sense into the boy."

He clears his throat, turns the page.

"What about your mother?"

"She's worried, like always. I'll head home after a week."

My aunt shakes her head.

"The way you are going, who knows what will happen?"

## The Monastery

The bus to the monastery leaves in the afternoon. I sit behind the rear door and gaze out the window as the road curves through hills covered with beech forests. Schoolchildren get off at each stop and run into houses with white walls, sloping red-tiled roofs, and black wrought-iron balconies crammed with flowerpots. Soon, the villages grow sparse and the bus is almost empty.

I try writing in my journal but can't concentrate. I pull out a map, spread it open on my lap, and trace the pilgrim route with a pen. The line starts in Roncesvalles, at a monastery near the French-Spanish border along the Pyrenees, then runs west for long stretches through open country dotted with small towns and occasionally through cities with names like Pamplona, Estella, Logroño, Burgos, León, and finally, Santiago de Compostela. It's about 780 kilometers long. Over five hundred miles. Much longer than my Italian friend's guess.

Am I crazy? I try remembering the last three months but the images blur: mountains, rivers, ashes. I'm not sure it meant anything at all. Now an eleventh-century pilgrim route in Spain.

"A pilgrimage?" I say, shaking my head. I almost want to laugh.

It is based on the story of Saint James, one of Christ's apostles, known in Spanish as Santiago, who was beheaded by King Herod and buried by his disciples in northwest Spain. The tomb was forgotten for centuries until a hermit shepherd followed a star in the night sky and discovered it. The place became known as Compostela, "field of stars."

The bus hits a bump, jolting me against the window. The sun is hidden by the hills, and past the initial line of trees, the woods are dark. The road climbs. The breeze, whistling through an open window up front, grows cooler.

When the Moors overran Spain, Christians needed a figure to rally around. There were reports of Santiago appearing all over Spain on a white horse, killing the invaders. The legend grew. A cathedral was built over his tomb and pilgrims arrived from all over Europe. The journey was called El Camino de Santiago, the road to Santiago.

For almost a thousand years, millions of pilgrims walked to the cathedral. But that was centuries ago. For all I know, the tradition has faded, and I might be one of a few on a long-forgotten journey.

"*Pardon,*" a man says. Strong French accent.

Outside, the trunks of the trees are white, their bottoms hidden by ferns, and branches arc out over the bus.

The man again. "You are a pilgrim?"

That gets my attention. He sits in the long rear seat. Late fifties, lean and handsome with graying hair, dark bushy eyebrows, and white stubble on his tanned face. He sticks his hands into the pockets of his faded hiking shorts and grins.

"Where is your stop?"

"Last one," I say. "The monastery in Roncesvalles."

He leans forward, shakes my hand. A strong, relaxed grip.

"We are both pilgrims. I'm Loïc."

"Amit," I say. "I don't think I qualify, though."

This makes him laugh. "It is not such a serious matter. If you are on the Camino, you are a pilgrim."

The bus slows, then stops outside a house. Vines cover the walls and the gate to the garden is red. A man gets off and we are the only passengers left. The bus starts again.

"How is your Spanish?" Loïc asks.

*"Pobre,"* I say. One class in college forever ago.

"Another not serious matter," he says. "Your French?"

"Nonexistent."

A mischievous grin. "That, I assure you, is a very serious matter."

Despite myself, I chuckle. He reaches into a white shopping bag and pulls out chorizo, *jamón serrano*, cheese, and bread, spreading them on the seat. My stomach rumbles. He fills two paper plates with food and passes one over.

"Eat," he says. "Unless you prefer to be an ascetic."

I thank him, then eat quietly. The bus passes no more villages, just shadows of trees on the road, shifting slightly in the wind. Sometimes, through the trees, I catch glimpses of pastures with grazing cattle, and, once, a field of rows and rows of sunflowers.

My mother loves sunflowers. I called her from the bus station in Barcelona, gave an edited version of my plans.

"I'm taking a group tour," I said. Much easier than explaining a pilgrimage I barely understood.

"Amit, you hate groups."

"Only one more week, Mom."

She sighed. "But you will do what you do. You are like me."

I think she might be getting used to my antics. She's had enough practice. Case in point, halfway through freshman year in college, I called her up.

"Mom, I'm thinking about joining the Army."

A long pause. "Be careful."

Two days later, another call.

"Mom. Guess what? I joined the Army."

The times when she does complain, I remind her of my history of off-the-cuff decisions.

"I am your mother," she reminds me in turn. "It's my job to worry."

According to my aunt, I've kept my poor mother working overtime.

"Be careful, okay?" she said when it was time to hang up. "Promise me. And return home soon."

I promised her the first. The second, I kept mum.

The shadow of the bus arches over a field, rises and falls over wheat stalks, then the trees close in again. For a moment, I'm struck by a strong desire to get off at the next stop, sprint to the nearest phone booth, and call my girlfriend. "It's beautiful, Sue," I want to tell her. "You'd love it." I want to share what I'm seeing. But the prospect of the conversation going where it went last time is enough to kill the urge. She couldn't understand that I didn't know when I'd be returning. The resulting argument was no fun. Simpler to just not call.

The bus passes a stone cross, about three feet high, at the entrance to a gravel path. The sides of the cross are blackened, as if by fire. Loïc taps my shoulder, handing me a plastic cup of red wine. As we drink, he fills me in on the Camino. The route we're headed for, the Camino Francés, is the most popular pilgrimage to Santiago de Compostela. But there are others, one from southern Spain, another from Portugal. Most important, he tells me that plenty of people come from all over the world to do this walk. Whether I like it or not, I won't be alone.

By our second cup, I already have a brief synopsis of his life. He comes from a long line of sailors in Brittany. He'd been a captain in the merchant marine, a professor of maritime studies, holds a doctorate in psychology, and now investigates maritime accidents for the European Union. "I work for Brussels," he says, shaking his head sadly whenever he mentions the EU. He loves Paris, jazz, and, more than anything, time on his sailboat.

"I bought my boat from an English naval officer. He told me that a sailor must choose between his boat and his wife." He smiles wistfully. "It appears that I chose the boat."

By the third cup, the scenery is sliding by the windows and we're liking each other pretty fine. I join him on the rear seat.

"Are you religious?" he asks.

"Far from it."

"Me also," he says. "I'm far too old for such matters. But look." He fishes a small paperback out of his cargo pocket, thumbs through it, and reads out loud. "If you bring forth what is within you, what you bring forth will save you. If you do not bring forth what is within you, what you do not bring forth will destroy you."

I let it sink in. If I do not bring forth what is within me, it will destroy me?

"Gospel of Thomas," he says.

"Can you tell me that again?"

No grin. Just a soft smile. He reads slowly. After he's finished, I am silent for a while.

"I've made the study of many things in my life," he says. "I have lived the lessons even less. The tragedy of life is not living what you know to be true." He raises a slight toast. "This is why I will walk the Camino. A start to a life of living the lessons. What is within me."

"That's beautiful," I say. "Really."

"And you?"

"An Italian told me that everyone who walks this finds themselves. So here I am."

He grins, reaches over and claps my shoulder.

"*Mon ami*, we will be good friends."

The bus downshifts loudly. We come up a steep hill, and as we crest, the spires and the gray stone buildings of the monastery appear. They have slanted metal roofs. Behind them, the hills grow higher and fold into the Pyrenees.

The driver pulls up in front of the largest building. Loïc goes out the rear door, and there is a bang against the side of the bus, then a creak. The driver opens the baggage hold. Loïc says something and the driver laughs. The Pyrenees remind me of the Himalayas behind the monk, what he'd said. I step out.

Loïc hands me my blue Lowe Alpine backpack. "Look at

that," he says, pointing to his pack. It looks like a cleaner version of mine. "We have the same."

"Sort of." I put it on and adjust the straps. "Mine's a fake."

"Sorry, what?"

"It's an imitation."

His dark eyebrows tighten and he looks like he's about to speak.

"My pack fell apart in India," I add. "On my way out, I bought this for very little money."

While he slips his arms through the thick, padded straps, I study his pack with its double-stitched, water-resistant lining. Mine has no lining and the straps are thin. I hope it lasts the week. The straps are already cutting into my shoulders and I don't want to think about how they will feel after an entire day.

Suited up, I follow him across the lawn to the far end of the building where a group of men and women wait outside a closed door. Most have backpacks. The others hold bicycles with satchels slung over the rear wheels.

There are nineteen of us, eleven men and eight women, ages ranging from twenties to sixties, everyone wearing different-colored versions of Gore-Tex. Except for me. I have on an imitation Patagonia fleece pullover I bought in India. Real cheap.

While he makes small talk with the others, I remove my pack and sit on it. Instead of joining the conversations, I am content to listen, maybe pick up more information. German, English, Spanish, Portuguese, French, and a few languages I can't place are spoken. There is one clear thing they have in common, though: their excitement.

The driver starts the bus up, turns it around slowly, and drives away. Soon it's gone and there is only the sound of pilgrims talking and the breeze through the trees lining the other side of the road. Seven days of this, then home. To Sue. To no clue what to do next.

A latch behind the door clicks and it swings open from inside. A line forms, me in the far back. We snake through the door, down a narrow hallway, and to an office, carrying our backpacks in our hands like suitcases. Past the heads, there is a woman with thick arms, her gray hair pulled up in a bun, sitting behind an oak desk. She smiles and waves us in. Bookcases line the walls and a framed print of the Virgin Mary hangs behind her.

The woman takes each person's name, writes it down in a ledger, and stamps a booklet they hold out. Her fingers are covered with streaks of blue ink.

"What's that?" I ask an Englishman in front of me.

"*Credencial,*" the man says, "pilgrim passport. You must get it stamped in the refuges."

"What's a refuge?" I ask.

He watches me for a moment, scratches his ear.

"Where were you planning on sleeping?"

"Youth hostels, cheap hotels. Maybe camp a few nights."

The line moves forward. I hear the hard thunk of the stamp on the desk. The woman stamps several booklets quickly. Thunk thunk thunk.

"No need for that," he says. "There's accommodations for pilgrims on the Camino. *Refugios.* Refuges. Some are rather nice, I hear. Then they've got your basic four-walls-and-a-roof types."

"Are they expensive?"

"Not if you've got a *credencial*."

The line moves again. Two thunks and he's gone.

Standing there, waiting my turn, I start to feel foolish. I really had no idea what this involved. The Englishman's boots, no scuffs, the laces still clean. Mine look like someone dragged them through the sewers of India. This helps me feel a little better. When I was in the Infantry, they didn't call us "legs" for nothing. I may not know the details of this pilgrimage, but I know how to walk.

The woman sells me a *credencial*. It's a long piece of cardstock folded several times like a map, each side divided into blank squares. She stamps the first square with a blue-inked image of the Virgin of Roncesvalles. I am now an official pilgrim.

Finished, she buttons up her brown sweater and motions for us to follow. We go out the door, through a stone court-yard, and inside another building. We walk up a winding stairway, the air growing colder, backpacks scraping the narrow walls, boots scuffling against stone steps.

The refuge is on the third floor. We claim bunks and a line forms for the single shower in the bathroom. I grab my journal, skip down the stairs past freshly arriving pilgrims, and head outside.

It's a cool evening. I do push-ups on the front grounds. Then, leaning on my elbows, I run my hands through the lush grass. The breeze ruffles my hair. Loïc joins me and we watch the sun dip low.

He pats my arm. "I like this very much."

Me too. No matter where in the world, you never tire of sunsets.

"You are a quiet fellow," he says. "Tell me, what is your profession?"

"Profession?" I noodle it over. "Unemployed, actually."

"A rather agreeable hobby," he says. "But in France, it is a rather serious matter, I can assure you. Everybody will be full of commiseration, speaking with the kind of voice you adopt when you shake hands with the widow after burying her husband."

I laugh, still nice and tipsy from the wine on our bus ride. "In the US, your friends give you high fives if you get more than two weeks' severance."

He looks at me closely, curious. "Tell me, your profession before this illustrious one?"

"Student," I say. "Somewhere right after graduating college, I decided I wanted to be a doctor, so I've been going part-time, taking all my pre-med courses and working as an aide in the emergency room."

"My ex-wife was a doctor," he says. "One needs remarkable dedication for such studies. I am impressed."

"Naah," I say. "I lost my job while wandering around, and honestly, I don't think I want to be a doctor anymore."

What I don't mention is the reason. Conversations are fine, sometimes even questions. Answers can always be tailored.

"Perhaps that is why you are on the Camino."

"I don't know. It's not like I have hard-and-fast reasons."

Biggest smile I've seen on his face so far. The man practically glows.

"Good," he says loudly. "Good. The heart, it does not listen to reason. It leads you into a fog. You do not know if you will fall off a cliff or it shall part and you are standing at the open gates to Shangri-La. But when you follow your heart, you are alive."

A thin gray cloud moves across the sun, cutting it in half, like a reflection in the water. We both fall quiet and watch the two halves slowly disappear behind the hills. When I blink, I see orange spots where the sun had been.

He waves an arm around. Then, quietly, "Reason did not bring you to this."

"True that," I say.

"Reason keeps you safe. This, this is not safe."

"Ah, how not safe?"

He waves it off. "Your heart brought you here. Would you like to know where it will take you?"

"Very much."

"Magic. That is the promise of the heart."

Not a word that's occurred to me, perhaps ever. We're both quiet for a while. Church bells ring, the sound echoing off the hills. We watch pilgrims file into the chapel. Loïc stands, holds a hand out.

"I thought you weren't religious," I say, letting him help me up.

"*Monsieur* American, we are on a pilgrimage."

"Fair enough." I pat grass off my jacket. "When in Rome."

He grins. "Do as the French."

We sit in a pew between giant, arched pillars. Three narrow, stained glass windows above the altar let in hints of dying light. As the bells quiet, monks in white robes file in. They gather along the steps to the altar in a straight line and chant. It is a long chant, growing louder, voices rising, until it fills the chapel. Sitting on a wooden pew next to a tipsy Frenchman, rubbing my hands together for warmth, watching the pilgrims around me, some kneeling, some moving their lips, and others like me, simply staring, I feel like I'm part of something bigger than just myself. I think I like it.

The chanting ends and it's time for communion. About half of the pilgrims, including Loïc, get in line, and after the last takes his seat, the monks raise their arms, palms facing forward. The one in the middle, bald with a neatly trimmed white beard, motions for us to come closer. He waits until we assemble in a semicircle, then speaks while one man translates into English, another into French.

"When you walk the Camino," he says, "you follow the footsteps of those who have come and gone. They sat where you sit. They stood where you stand. Remember them, and one day, others will remember you."

In the bunkroom, the woman who stamped the *credenciales* had remarked that today's group was a small one. Each morning, a new group would start at Roncesvalles, while others started at different cities along the Camino, some walking from as far as France or Holland. She told us about a bridge at a village called Puente la Reina where several pilgrim routes converged into one.

There would be moments, she'd said, when we would be completely alone with no one around, and then, times when we would be surrounded by pilgrims, just one of many. The way she smiled when she said that, she almost made it sound like a good thing.

The monk gazes at us for a long, silent moment, as if searching for someone familiar. A woman behind me coughs.

"Pray for us when you reach Santiago," he finally says.

The monks lower their arms, turn, and retreat, candles flickering their shadows on the walls. As the chapel empties, I open my journal. At the airport in New Delhi, my aunt pressed the small leather-bound notebook into my hands. "For you," she'd said, hugging me goodbye. "Don't get lost." She watched me flip through the blank pages, then gently rubbed my cheek. Sitting inside a fourteenth-century chapel in Spain, preparing to follow the footsteps of long-dead pilgrims, I find myself missing her.

Maybe I should have answered her questions. He was her only brother. She had a right to know. I write down what the monk said. A habit I've developed while traveling—soak in wherever you are because you may never be back. A monk returns to the altar and picks up a candle. He is small and thin and very old. How many pilgrims has he watched setting off for Santiago? We make eye contact for a moment, then he shuffles to the side entrance and shuts the door behind him. I walk out.

A few stars appear above, faint in the darkening sky. A low mist covers the hills. It's dinnertime. I join Loïc at a communal table in the crowded and noisy restaurant. Rough stone walls, casks of wine behind the bar, candles on the tables, fluorescent lights on the ceiling, and a waitress who looks like she's waited on too many pilgrims in her lifetime, serving bread, salad, and fried trout.

Loïc holds court, laughing, chewing loudly, talking with the women in French, making them laugh. He jokes with the men and refills my glass every chance he gets. By the time we have coffee and flan for dessert, there are batches of empty wine bottles on the table.

If someone asked me to imagine pilgrims, this wouldn't be it. Church groups, yes. Solemn and quiet, sure. Laughter and drunkenness, no.

The group orders another round of wine. The conversation turns deeper, people sharing why they're here. I excuse myself and leave behind the noise, the cigarette smoke, and the reasons. The lawn is deserted and the monastery quiet. When I finally reach the bunkroom, the lights are off and a man snores loudly. A couple sits on the floor, whispering in Spanish.

By the open window, the cold air numbs my face. The hills are dark lumps. I zip up my fleece pullover. The moonless night sky glitters, and soon the mind falls quiet.

A January night in New York. In a small hospital room in Long Island Jewish Medical Center. Outside the window, snow, brown and dirty from the street, piled against sidewalks. Inside, neither hot nor cold. Hospital weather.

On the bed lay the body of what used to be my father. The cancer had left darkened, brown skin draped over bones. From his mouth, a tube coiled itself into a machine that mimicked his lungs, forcing him to breathe. His head remained still but his eyes moved around and around, rolling, searching. They took in everything: the yellow ceiling, the plastic jug half full of urine, the white sheets, the door leading into a pale corridor where nurses in blue scrubs walked by, the son who sat by him. They kept on moving, searching, seeking.

"A primitive reaction of the brain," the neurologist said while suctioning electrodes to my father's head. "It means nothing."

Wires ran from the electrodes to a boxy, antiquated machine with flashing buttons. Green wires. Red wires. White and yellow wires. An absurd Christmas tree.

Yet, I saw the eyes. Only the eyes. Rolling, flittering, moving, searching, endlessly searching. What were they looking for?

I stood, looked down at him. I could kill him. Not the first time in my life, this thought. But now, simple: block the door, unplug the ventilator, put a pillow over his face, end the misery.

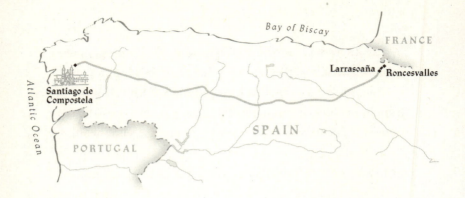

## Day One

Bright blue sky, puffs of clouds to the west. The air is cool and smells of freshly cut grass. Behind me are the Pyrenees, their edges crisp in the morning light. Sheep graze on a slope.

On the road, a yellow arrow is painted lengthwise on a small signpost. It points to a dirt trail that runs adjacent to the road for about fifty yards, then veers into the forest. Last night, during dinner, Loïc spoke about the tradition of yellow arrows marking the route to Santiago, on rocks, trees, signposts, sidewalks. As long as you followed them, you knew that you were on the Camino de Santiago.

I take a deep breath, feel my chest expand, let it out slowly. Beginnings are the most exciting moments. They're also the scariest. The Italian backpacker who seeded this journey had told me his favorite legend, an Indian one. The night before he achieved enlightenment, the Buddha was attacked by Mara, the God of Death. He threw everything he had—lust, greed, anger, doubt, fear in all its forms—at the man meditating under the tree. No luck.

But even after he lost, he continued showing up throughout Buddha's life. Each time, the Buddha said, "I see you, Mara." That's it.

The genius of this, the Italian said, was in the simplicity. He named fear for what it was, acknowledged its existence, and then just let it be. That took away Mara's power, which was an illusion anyway. Eventually, Mara grew bored and wandered away.

I'd forgotten the story until now. Funny, I need to be in Spain to appreciate what I learned in India.

"I see you, Mara," I whisper. "I see you."

Then I shoulder my pack, tighten the straps, clip the waist belt. Twenty-five hundred years ago, Lao Tzu said, "The longest journey beings with a single step." Mine starts on a paved road outside a monastery in the hills of northern Spain. It curves into a forest path where a streaky yellow arrow points into the foliage. Tall, skinny trees with white trunks reach toward each other, forming a shady canopy of green. I walk slowly to an unfamiliar rhythm, map in one hand, searching for arrows. The sound of my boots on the sandy trail fades into the hills.

For almost an hour, I see no one. Not surprising, given that they were long gone by the time I woke. Still, it's perfect: a sunny morning, a cool breeze, the smell of ferns and beeches, the shifting of the straps on the shoulders, the sound of water sloshing in a bottle in my pack, the mind still, the body moving.

The path stays in the forest until the village of Burguete. Then I'm on a paved road lined with houses with whitewashed walls and bright red shutters. Two pilgrims from Roncesvalles rest on a bench across the street, their backpacks on the pavement. Scallop shells dangle around their necks—the symbol of the Camino. Ancient pilgrims carried them to scoop water from streams and rivers. Modern pilgrims use them as a badge. We wave but I don't join them. I want to make up for my late start and catch up with Loïc.

A yellow arrow on the sidewalk leads away from the road and down a muddy footpath. The sky is now a light gray and the clouds are darker and closer. The mud on the trail grows softer and leads into a beech forest. I'm alone again until I hear the sounds of cars through the trees, like a distant waterfall. Soon, the path intersects a paved road and Loïc is on the other side, taking photos of a statue of the Virgin of Roncesvalles.

He waves me over. We walk to an opening in the trees, set our packs down, and, just like in the bus, he pulls out fruit and cheese for lunch. The man is a walking picnic basket. Unlike yesterday, he's subdued, probably hungover. I know I am. So we eat in silence.

Then we lie in the grass, watch the sun stream through the clouds as it warms our faces. A cricket chirps lazily. Not so bad, this Camino thing. New friend or two, easy hiking, siestas, and after seven days, veer off to home.

"Hey, Loïc."

"*Oui?*"

"The magic thing from yesterday. A quick question."

"Yes. Of course."

"Fog parting to Shangri-La, I get it. Nice metaphor. But falling off a cliff, how's that a good thing?"

He laughs. "Actually, *mon ami*, it is the best thing. You grow wings."

The man has a solution for everything.

"I will tell you," he says, "this is a very important moment. You are at the edge of a cliff and you stand and wait for wings to grow before you jump." He sits up to face me. "But life wants you to jump first, then your wings grow. And I assure you, they grow quickly."

He lifts a palm up, then drops it fast. A smile.

"Because, well, the ground."

"A sort of faith?"

"It is how life works." He shrugs. "I don't know why."

"So either way," I say, "cliff or Shangri-La, you've got—"

"Magic."

Then he's quiet. The clouds drift. Leaves rustle.

"You're pretty low-key today," I say.

"Well, it is my birthday."

"Hey. Happy Birthday!"

"It was my wish to contemplate on the Camino today."

By now I should have picked up on it. Traveling hones your sense of when someone wants to be left alone. Unless you're me, apparently. I sit up and reach for my pack. He looks grateful.

"Will you celebrate tonight?"

"At my age, the desire to celebrate is not so strong."

"Well, contemplation is a sort of celebration."

He looks pleased. Best to leave on this note.

"The gift of age," he says. "You understand your own hypocrisy. This makes it easier to forgive others. But you have to forgive yourself as well. That is not always so easy."

I catch myself frowning. He smiles, slightly embarrassed.

"*À bientôt,*" he says, handing me a peach. "For your journey today."

"Happy birthday, my friend."

Back in the forest, the trail narrows, the sounds of cars fade, and the canopy grows dense. Far through the trees, the land falls sharply into a valley crisscrossed with sandy white roads.

I hook my thumbs through the straps on my chest and pull forward, lightening the load on my shoulders. At the restaurant last night, when drunken pilgrims started sharing their reasons for this walk, all seemed to be going through something. Do any happy people do this thing?

The trail starts to twist, then climbs a steep angle. Sharp rocks, some the size of bricks, others like boulders, jut through the ground. Clouds slowly block the sun. The wind rushes through the branches, making the pines tremble. At the crest of a hill, I slip on a moss-covered rock, barely grabbing hold of a bush to stop myself from tumbling down the slope.

Farther below, is a slim figure wearing blue shorts, a white T-shirt, and a light blue backpack. But it isn't the appearance of another pilgrim that catches my eye; it is the way she maneuvers down the hill. While I slide and pick my way through the rocks, she walks down like they don't exist. In a hurry to catch up, I fall again, this time landing hard on my back, my pack underneath me.

I lie there for a moment, wondering what I'm doing here, where my life is going, why am I not relaxing on a nice, warm beach somewhere, why oh why do I have to be me and choose these crazy things? After a couple minutes, I check myself. A few scratches, a bruised ego. The woman is watching. I brush myself off and carefully make my way down.

"Hi again," I say, reaching her.

Tanned, with short, dark hair, fine laugh lines. Probably a few years older than me. Silver dangling earrings in the shape of dolphins, intense hazel eyes. There's something about the way she stands, her poise—you can't quite put a finger on it, but once you notice, you can't look away.

She was at the far end of the table at dinner, a Brazilian named Roseangela. I'd been too lost in myself to pay her much attention. Or anyone, for that matter.

"Are you well?"

I point to my mud-covered pants. "I've been better."

She giggles, covers her mouth. "I heard you fall."

"Oh, that?" I scrape dirt off my cheek. "Just a little spill."

She laughs a soft laugh. The dolphins shake. "It sounded like a big spill."

As we head downhill, I—Mister Infantry guy who once climbed mountains in the Army—use my hands and feet for leverage against the rocks while she walks like the terrain was designed for her. She does not slip once. I, on the other hand, almost meet my maker several times.

The trail widens into a clearing and to our right is a two-arched stone bridge. Power lines dip from wooden poles on both sides of the stream. We pause for a break.

"You hike a lot?" I ask.

"It is my first time that I have done such a thing."

"Seriously?"

She nods. "I was worried how it might be. But it is wonderful, don't you think?"

"As long as you don't fall."

She laughs again. This time at me, I think.

Past the bridge, over the rise of a hill, is a small village.

"I will rest for a few minutes," she says, and I get the same feeling as with Loïc. Makes sense, walking alone on the first day, getting a feel for a brand-new journey, the whole contemplation thing.

"See you at the refuge," I say.

She smiles gently. All the way from her eyes to the corners of her mouth.

A yellow arrow on a boulder returns me into the forest. The sky grows grayish, dark. I put on a poncho and increase my pace. The branches start swaying wildly. Leaves and twigs swirl in the wind. There is a loud ripping sound, the clinks of pebbles, then hailstones pelt my head. Soon, sheets of rain fall and my boots sink into the trail, slowing me down. I half walk, half stumble, one hand holding down my poncho hood, squinting into the rain.

The trail narrows to a footpath to an open meadow. The rain is sideways. Lightning strikes a hill near the horizon, an eerie bluish-white flash blinds me. Seconds later, muffled thunder. Then another strike, this time closer. Thunder crackles and rolls through the hills. My God, this whole thing sucks.

At the bridge into Larrasoña, the rain slows to a drizzle. The stream is brown, the water fast-moving. The bottoms of the clouds are tinged with red. My boots are caked in mud. A road sign gives the name of the village and the distance to Santiago: 760 kilometers. Now the pilgrims' reasons from last night make sense. You'd have to be seriously unhappy to put yourself through a month of this. I can't even imagine six more days.

The refuge is a two-story white building with a small fountain out front. I rub the mist off my watch: 6:42 p.m. Over ten hours of walking.

I follow two men with backpacks to a laundry sink behind the building to wash our boots and ponchos. The drizzle lightens. Clouds roll down the hills, covering the slopes. Sometimes the wind uncovers the pines and patches of green show. The air is clean, and occasionally, when the wind shifts, I smell woodsmoke. My body aches, there are raw marks on my shoulders from the straps, and my ankles hurt with each step. Still, after a day like today, a simple view and sneakers on your feet instead of boots is enough.

A group gathers around the sink, talking loudly, comparing stories of their first day and their accounts of aches, pain, blisters. Those I can identify with. When they get to their reasons for doing this walk, how long they planned it, some even waiting for years, they lose me. I don't belong here.

The *hospitalero*, the man who runs the refuge, is in the lounge, shouting, clapping pilgrims on the back, his large stomach leading his body. He's also, according to a pilgrim outside, mayor of Larrasoña. In his office, the walls are covered with photos of pilgrims who stopped here. Books, pamphlets, stickers—anything to do with the Camino de Santiago—clutter his desk.

Felipe, a pilgrim from Madrid, walks in with the mayor. He guides him toward three framed certificates on the wall above his desk.

"What are those?" I ask.

"*Compostelas,*" Felipe says. "It shows that you completed the pilgrimage. He has walked the Camino three times."

The top of each certificate is an image of a pilgrim in a robe carrying a staff with a gourd. The writing is in Latin. On the bottom, an image of a scallop shell. I turn to the mayor.

"Three?"

He straightens and nods proudly, as if I just complimented his war medals. That kills the urge to ask why do this more than once. I have a feeling that every visitor to the refuge is shown these *compostelas*. Then again, if this first day with its rocks, mud, hailstones, lightning, and almost-twisted ankles is any indication of the rest, he's more than earned it.

I sign the register and pay the fee. He stamps my *credencial* with the crest of Larrasoña, signs his name underneath, then grabs my hands, squeezes them tight and says, *"Buen viaje."* He lets go and sells me a scallop shell to hang on my pack. He signs that also.

While pilgrims head out to explore the village, I go and lean on the railing outside the front door. Raindrops slide along the smooth metal. The pilgrims walk down the street, sandals flapping against wet cobblestone.

The mayor, now without an audience, comes out and joins me. He slaps my back, points up at the hills, and talks about his childhood. He tells me about his youth, when he watched pilgrims pass by, the three times he walked the Camino, and how he wept each time he reached the cathedral in Santiago. He talks about his life in the fields, where he worked like his father and his father before him. His voice falls for the first time when he mentions his children and grandchildren, to whom he will pass on the legacy of caring for pilgrims.

At least that's what I hope he said. I couldn't understand a word that came from his mouth. For all I know, he could've been insulting my looks, my family, and the land where I was from.

When he lowered his voice, he might have been despairing the fact that I was ever born and now breathed the same air he did.

It doesn't matter. I like this man who lives in a little village in the hills and serves pilgrims he's never met before. He has found his place in the world. I admire him for that.

The mayor frowns and glances at his watch, then slaps the railing.

"*Mira.*" He points at the street.

Pilgrims are rounding the corner. He's found a larger audience to entertain. He laughs, shouts, drinks wine with us while we eat dinner in a restaurant. Then he shakes our hands one by one and leaves.

Thunder booms over the roofs in a series of echoes. It starts raining again. Holding newspapers over our heads, we run to the refuge. While pilgrims go to sleep, I relax on a couch in the office and read. The window is open and the breeze smells of the earth. Felipe is at a table in the corner, writing in a notebook. His gray hair is slicked back, wet from the famous hot showers pilgrims stood in line for. The desk lamp casts his shadow on the wall.

After a while, he leans back in the chair and yawns.

"What are you reading?"

I hold the book up, a gift from my aunt at the airport.

"The *Gita.*"

The teachings of my ancestors, she'd said, pressing it in my hands at the security line, then made me swear up and down that I would read it. My coming to India proved to her that, no matter how I felt, if I made a promise, I kept it.

"Interesting. Would you share a little?"

The title: "Final Revelations of the Ultimate Truth."

"All of these acts should be performed
renouncing the attachment to the fruit of actions."

"Without aversion to unpleasant work
and without attachment to pleasant work,
the renouncer is intelligent and free
from all doubts."

He taps on his notebook, thinks for a moment.

"Good advice on walking the Camino."

I imagine my aunt hearing this and saying, "Of course. Our people invented pilgrimages." That makes me laugh.

"And for your search."

"My search?"

"Last night, what you said to that Frenchman, the choice you wish to make regarding a career."

Now I remember him listening intently to my conversation with Loïc over dinner. He'd wanted to know why I didn't want to be a doctor anymore, and I'd managed to sidestep it, saying I just wasn't sure it was right for me.

"Oh, that? No big deal, just trying to figure things out."

He shakes his head. "No, no. It is a most important decision."

"I guess."

"When I started my education, I was a student of physics. But I left physics and went to management school in the States and joined my father's business." He sighs. "Opportunities. We should study them carefully to see where they will lead."

Past the window, hills light up in quick flashes of white. Seconds later, all the windowpanes rattle.

"I have done well," he continues, "good business, good family, a comfortable life. But the more time passes, the more I hate my work. I would much rather sit in my office and dream of atoms."

He walks to another window, opens it, and stares out at the night. The cross-ventilation feels good and I finish the last chapter. When he returns, he pulls the chair closer and sits, leaning toward me.

"Listen, I will tell you something. Dr. Richard Feynman came to lecture at my university. This is when I was still in physics. He was a very famous scientist, an American. It was an honor to learn from him." His voice grows excited. "Dr. Feynman was the most curious man I have ever met. Always asking, 'What if you did this?' 'What does this mean?' 'Why, why?' For him, questioning was like breathing."

He yawns, crosses his arms.

"Now I realize, that was Dr. Feynman's secret. He chose for a profession what came to him naturally. After all, physics is just the asking of questions." He shrugs, then smiles. "Dr. Feynman must have been a happy man."

One time Sue visited me at work in the emergency room. Ever since then, she encouraged me to follow through on medical school. She said that I was more natural and relaxed around patients than anywhere else. She would have enjoyed what Felipe just said.

"Thanks for sharing this," I say. "It's good to know."

He doesn't miss a beat.

"Knowing is nothing unless you take on doing it."

The ceiling creaks with the sound of someone walking above. The rain grows louder. He stands up, gathers his things. I give him the *Gita*. Books should be shared, not hoarded.

# Day Two

In 1961, the Soviets took a man named Yuri Gagarin, strapped him inside a Vostok rocket, and shot him into outer space. As he orbited Earth, he looked out of his window and saw continents and cloud-covered oceans drifting below. He knew where his journey began and where it would end. At seventeen thousand miles per hour in a tin can, he had perspective.

All I see is a wet, slippery, two-lane highway curving through granite cliffs. Second day on the Camino, walking along the edge of the road. On one side, fields of wheat bend in the wind. On the other, wisps of fog roll down cliffs. Large trucks drive by, their tires spraying my poncho and soaking me below the knees. Red poppies in the fields droop, water dripping from their petals.

I want to reach shelter, dry off, drink something warm, get this day over with.

"Hello," someone says, breathless. It's a poncho-clad Roseangela.

"Hey, where did you come from?"

She points behind her.

"You could have shouted," I say. "I would have waited."

A truck rounds the bend and we turn to face the fields. The spray hits our backs like pellets.

"You would hear me in *this*?"

"Good point."

We walk at a slow pace. Three pilgrims, wearing yellow garbage bags as ponchos, speed past us. Roseangela waves.

"Do you know what is special about this Camino?" she asks.

I make a show of glancing around. "The weather?"

She laughs. The dolphins tremble under her poncho hood. "We are searching, all searching for something. This makes us a little crazy. You have to be crazy to travel to a foreign country and walk eight hundred kilometers, no?"

"Crazy, true."

"We may be different, you from New York, me from São Paulo, but down inside, we have one thing in common—we are searching. It is very special, very unique."

A car drives by, headlights flashing on and off. A hello of sorts. Or perhaps a what-the-heck-are-you-fools-doing? The three pilgrims are already small specks.

"My search," Roseangela says quietly, gazing at the fields. "You already know."

I nod. Last night over dinner, when the conversation turned once again to why pilgrims were here, she shared freely about the end of her engagement, the resulting heartbreak. The fine lines edged along her eyes aren't all from smiles.

"We Brazilians are an open people," she'd said to us. "It's our culture. That is why I'm on the Camino. My heart is closed and I wish for it to open."

This was shortly before I excused myself from the table.

"It is difficult to be away from my family," she says. "But I know that when I return, I will have more to give. I will be a better woman, a better daughter."

"You don't seem so bad. Not that I know you as a daughter, that is."

This makes her laugh. I like it when she laughs. Her eyes blink, the dolphins dance, and the sound is soft and musical and there is nothing fake about it.

"Thank you," she says. "And you, what is your search?"

"Beats me," I say, just a bit too quickly.

She tilts her head, watches me. A long moment passes. Raindrops patter on my poncho.

"You will find it." She turns to the road. "Whatever we do, we must not let this experience pass us by. It must leave a mark. It has to."

We walk for a while, see signs for Pamplona, each one bringing us closer to the city. A city with a refuge, warmth, wine, and, I hope, the Spanish equivalent of chicken soup. The rain slows, then stops. We remove our ponchos and hang them on our packs. She unzips her jacket, shakes her head side to side, drops of water flying from her hair.

"I would like to have come next year," she says, "but my heart."

"What's next year?"

"Well, when you walk the Camino, it will cut your time

in purgatory by half. But if you come on a holy year—next year—all your sins are forgiven. It is very special and people come from all over the world."

"I'm only here for a week, will I get a fourth off?"

She laughs that singsong laugh again.

"Perhaps I will return," she says. "My heart will be open. When you fall in love, does it not always feel like the first time? Perhaps by then, I shall be loving again."

I could hang out with this woman all day and be just fine, even with wet clothes and aching lower back. I smile.

The highway winds through the hills, then into a small city with crowded sidewalk cafés, concrete office buildings, and traffic. Soon they give way to a stone bridge and Pamplona.

The ancient walls make it look like a medieval fortress, though these days all they protect are, as a passing pilgrim points out, more than seven hundred bars. That qualifies it for a pilgrimage of its own.

We are on a narrow street. Cars and scooters weave through pedestrians. We pass food stalls, markets, restaurants, and shops with steamy windows. The smells shift and change and mingle. Olives, sausages, oils, and spices.

"Why a week?" Roseangela asks, breaking her silence. "You have to return for your job?"

"No. No big reason."

"But the Camino is so special," she says. "Why would you not finish?"

"I hadn't thought of it that way. I just can't imagine walking across a whole country. I don't see the point."

She purses her lips, sighs. "What is the point of this...this walking for a week?"

The way she says it causes my jaw to tighten.

"I'm sorry." She gently touches my hand. "I am being forward and—"

"It's all right." A long pause. "This seemed like a great excuse to get away from where I was. But I think I'm tired of drifting."

A ham leg hangs behind a darkened store window. It looks lonely. Probably misses the other three.

"What do you run from?"

That catches me off guard. I shrug.

"From what?" Her face is closer. Raindrops glisten on her cheeks. "Running or searching, it is often the same."

Cars drive past but I can't hear them anymore. I only see a faint hint of my reflection in her hazel eyes and say the first thing that comes to mind. "Memories."

She blinks. For a brief moment, my reflection disappears. That snaps me out of wherever I was.

"*Your* heart," she says, softly. A look of understanding. "*Saudade.*"

"What?"

"*Saudade*. A word that only exists in Portuguese. When you feel *saudade*, all the things and feelings you shared with a person come to you."

"Nice word." I face forward. "Not what I'm talking about."

"Well." She nods. "I will not be surprised to see you in Santiago. The Camino, it becomes a part of you. Yes, I see it. It wi—"

"I've only been here two days."

"It does not matter. I see it."

"All I've seen is rain."

She smiles but doesn't say anything. We leave it at that.

Most of the bunks in the refuge are already taken. Sleeping bags are rolled over mattresses and the large room smells like drying socks. We find two bunks near each other, lie down to rest, and listen to the sounds of the city through the window, the sounds of people stumbling in and out of seven hundred bars.

Eventually, I grow bored and go out to explore the famous Plaza de Toros, the bullfighting ring. Outside the gates, a statue of Ernest Hemingway, the writer who made this city world famous. He looks sad, sort of like the ham leg.

"I know how you feel." I run a hand over his stone shoulder. "Movement sure beats sitting still."

I think back to a lazy afternoon in New Delhi, resting in my aunt's garden, writing in my journal, wondering how long to stay, what it might be like to finally return home. Bangles clinked softly. I glanced up. My aunt sat down on the grass, folded her legs to the side, and leaned into me. The corners of her eyes were wet.

"Did he," she said, then hesitated. I shut the journal. "Was there…" Her hand brushed mine. "Did he suffer?"

I straightened and our eyes met. A thin band of muscle along her neck quivered slightly. So far, I'd managed to avoid conversations about my father, but now it hit me: he wasn't just my father. He was her brother.

"You have your mother's beauty," she said quietly, running her fingers along my cheek, "and your father's eyes."

The thin body in the hospital bed, skin like old linen, the skeleton hollowed by bone cancer, the eyes moving. The same eyes that, as a child, terrified me with their drunken anger. I didn't want his eyes.

"No," I said. "He was okay, he didn't suffer much."

She stared at me long and hard and something in her eyes shifted. I was never a good liar anyway. Her face softened and she almost smiled.

"He would be proud of you." She reached over, held my hand, her palm squeezing mine. "He loved you very much."

I opened my journal and flipped through the pages. It was almost full. I could hear the drumbeat of my heart in my ears. Could she feel it through the veins in my wrist?

"You are his child." I felt her grip tighten. "You were there? You took care of him?"

I shrugged, said, "A little," and felt the guilt in my stomach open like a flower and rot, a burning sensation. How could I explain to his sister that since my parents' divorce when I was twelve, I'd cut him off from my life until he was dying and even then couldn't allow myself to get close?

She searched my face, as if the answers were there. Painted on the inside of my lips, hidden behind the eyebrows, tucked deep within the folds of the ears. A treasure that, if she looked closely enough, would appear. Why had her brother died? How badly did he suffer? Why did his only child refuse to talk about him? You are looking in the wrong place, I thought, I have shut the lid on my memories. You will find no answers here.

My aunt started speaking, her voice low and faraway-sounding, as if talking to herself, reliving memories of a brother who died in a foreign land. She spoke of things I never knew: the two of them, little children, swimming in streams swollen from monsoon rains, running through mango groves, playing hide-and-seek, the wind in their dark hair, tears of laughter, her tying a colorful thread, a *rakhi*, on his wrist.

He always wanted to be a singer, she said. He loved her homemade mango chutney; she sent him jars of it for each birthday. When he was fifteen, a friend from school died in a car accident, and for months afterward, he would walk daily to the parents' house, three miles each way, and comfort them.

Quietly, softly, as if in an afterthought, she mentioned how he protected her when their father beat them. That shook me. My father, my grandfather, these generations of men that led to me, all making the same mistakes. My aunt watched me closely.

"He was a good man," she said. "Inside, a good man."

I didn't reply. No nod. Nothing.

Near the edge of the garden wall, a white lotus grew among dry leaves in a small pond. The breeze picked up, the pond rippled, and leaves spiraled around the flower. Then she spoke of things I already knew, some better than her: how my father left India with dreams of a prosperous life, saving enough money to bring my mother over two years later. He ran an import-export business until it failed when I was three. Jobs he held, then couldn't. She mentioned my mother, that she understood why we left my father.

"How is she?" she asked.

"Fine," I said. "I called her yesterday. She's worried about me, the usual. She sends her love."

She nodded. "He should have stayed here, with his people." She swallowed hard. "He would not have drank. Not here."

"It's too late to change anything," I wanted to say. The man I knew drank and beat his wife and son. And even when the cancer was killing him, I couldn't let go of the past. He's dead now. Dead. Dead. Dead. Everything's too late.

I stood up but she held on to my hand.

"He always wanted you to see India."

"He did?" I asked. That surprised me.

"Yes. You did not know?"

I shook my head. If he'd asked me to see the land of his birth, I would have refused. But by bringing his ashes here, then wandering around, that was exactly what had happened. Maybe he started the journey, but the rest is mine to create.

Streetlights blink on, profiling Hemingway, making him look sadder than before. I wander through Pamplona, pass the closed tourist office, sit on a bench in the main square. The stories Hemingway told, the life he lived, all of it ended with a squeeze of a finger on a trigger. What else could he have done if he had put the shotgun down, gone back to bed? What would he have learned in that moment of choosing to live, what other books would have been written?

Meanwhile, my father clung to life, putting his faith in doctors and chemotherapy and radiation, and all that time, the cancer like a swarm of termites, consuming his body while he slept. Even that last night, while his organs slowly shut down and he couldn't speak or hear, he hung on until I reached the hospital. Why? What makes one man, all alone in a foreign land, hang on, while another, with his fame and accomplishments and accolades, chooses a different path?

The wooden slats are damp and cold through the T-shirt on my back. I suddenly feel it, this exhaustion that's been building over the months. From the aimless wandering. These questions upon questions but no answers. This can't go on much longer.

I return to an empty refuge, everyone out for dinner. Perfect. Alone time. I do several rounds of push-ups, then take a long and delicious hot shower. Towel around my waist, not expecting anyone around, I walk out of the bathroom and there she is in her bunk, Roseangela, eating a sandwich and writing in her journal.

I feel her eyes on me. She catches herself, starts scribbling fast. Nonchalantly, I walk to my bunk and throw clothes on. Then, time for a dinner of hard cheese and bread I bought in Larrasoña. It's no chicken soup, but at least I'm warm and clean.

A church bell clangs, deep and hollow. Roseangela is on her stomach, knees folded, the bare soles of her feet facing the ceiling. She's flipping through her journal. The overhead light casts shadows around us.

"What'd you write about?" I ask.

"About the early pilgrims, how they suffered." She points with the pen to the wet ponchos and backpacks lined against a wall. "They did not have these. Do you know what they carried? A staff, a gourd, and a scallop shell. And their faith. When they finished, they walked back to their homes."

Insane. Yet, they had direction. No making up the journey as they went along.

"It is humbling," she says. "They had so little, we have so much. Still, it is their footsteps we follow."

I sit up, dangle my legs over the floor.

"They just walked west, huh?"

"So many robbed. So many beaten and killed. But they left their mark."

"Crazy," I say quietly. "Amazing."

"Yes," she says. "Now it is our turn."

Direction, purpose. What had they found?

She raps her pen on the journal loudly, smiles at me.

"Your turn."

I grin. "Dream on."

She laughs. "We will see, my pilgrim. We will see."

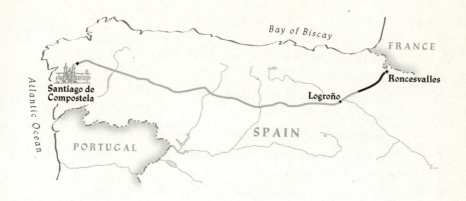

## Day Four

On the edge of a dirt trail, I eat an apple for breakfast, watching the sun rise. It is high up, surrounded by hills, and, far below, a river curves through fields. Daylight spreads across the valley floor, passes through a village, turns houses and church spires bright orange, climbs up the hillside. The river sparkles.

I was writing in my journal in an outdoor café in that village, when I noticed a woman drinking a glass of white wine at our communal table. Midfifties, face slightly sunburned; wavy, shoulder-length brown hair, graying around the temples; sharp wrinkles around eyes and lips. Her boots were muddy and her eyes were a deep blue.

She gently kissed the back of her own hand. I couldn't help but watch and she caught me.

"Nice to meet you," she said. Beautiful French accent, her voice almost a whisper.

I gave an embarrassed hello.

"I do it daily," she said. "Mostly in the morning when I wake."

"Can I ask why?"

"It is giving myself love. Like to a baby. Pure love."

I stared at her.

"Try it," she said. "It will change your life."

"I don't think life's that simple," I said.

She laughed at me.

"You have no idea," she said, shaking her head. "You have no idea."

She slowly unrolled her scarf, set it aside, and looked at me with a quiet strength. There were long sharp scars across her throat, like slashes. She saw my face.

"Cancer."

I swallowed hard. "I'm sorry."

To my surprise, she smiled. "No, no. It gave me my life."

"Your life?"

"It gave me notice. To live."

Then, she drank her white wine and told me her story.

"Ten years ago," she said, "I was told that I would die."

A successful lawyer who lived on one of the most expensive streets in Paris, she was forced to look at her life with the ferocity of one who knows that there isn't much time left.

"Most of my life," she said, "I was my worst enemy. Then the cancer gave me a gift in the form of a question. It might be too simple for you."

She stopped and chuckled.

"Would you like to hear it?"

"Very much."

"Here: 'If I loved myself, what would I do?'"

"You're right," I said. "That is simple."

"Notice the question has an 'if.' It never assumes that I do. Just 'if.' So I could ask no matter if I was in pain or laughing or crying. Just 'if.' "

She took a long swallow.

"I asked and I asked and I asked and it stopped all the behavior that impeded me. I never had to do anything. Just answer this one question."

She left her career, disassociated from people, threw away possessions. Anything she felt would hold her back was gone.

"I did not choose friends anymore for their status. I started to choose friends who made me happy. Everything I did, from eating and drinking to where I live, all through this one question. I believe we are all connected, so it was good for everyone around me, too."

"The ripple effect," I said. "When you throw a rock into a pond, the ripples go far beyond the original impact."

Now she ran a house for the homeless in Paris and was walking the Camino to celebrate her life. She had survived thirteen surgeries in ten years and knew that she could die at any time. The cancer still lurked like an old childhood fear, refusing to let go. But the same disease that threatened to destroy her had also set her free.

"It does not matter if I die two months from now," she said, drinking the last of her wine. "What matters is that I have lived the last ten years the way I wanted to."

Her words haunt me a day later. Sunlight streams through the clouds, causing sections of the village to glow.

"Today," she said when we parted, "I am my best friend."

"The question became your yellow arrow," I said. This pleased her so much, she gave me a tight hug.

I stretch my neck, put the pack on, tighten the straps. Ahead, the trail climbs sharply up a hill where a row of tall, white windmills dot the crest. The arms rotate slowly. I feel like Don Quixote, sans Sancho, horse, or lance.

The breeze picks up, ruffles my hair. *Cafuné*, another word Roseangela taught me, Brazilian for the act of tenderly running your fingers through someone's hair. *Cafuné*, I say to the wind and know who I'm thinking of. I have a phone call to make.

# Day Five

In the city of Logroño, I find a phone booth and wedge myself and my pack through the folding glass door. It's early afternoon and hazy, white clouds dodge the sun. Sue should be sleeping right now, but I want to tell her I'm returning, that I am an official pilgrim. That'll make her laugh.

I punch in the numbers. A click, a series of touch-tones, a pause, then the phone rings. One ring. Two rings. Three. And suddenly memories and feelings come rushing through: how she slept next to me, her hands pulled close to her face, breathing softly. Sometimes I'd wake up to find her watching me. She would smile and say, "You sleep so quiet, like a baby," and then she would softly kiss my forehead, my cheekbones, my eyes, my lips. Finished, she would snuggle in and put her head on my chest. I'd hold her tight and we'd fall asleep.

*Saudade*. She picks up on the fifth ring.

"Hi, it's me."

After all these months, this is my monumental greeting. An awkward moment of silence.

"Oh, hi. Where are you?"

"Spain. I'm on a pilgrimage."

In the background, through the receiver, through the cables buried deep in the Atlantic, through the phone lines snaking their way underneath the streets of Manhattan, the muffled voice of a man. The bed creaks. He moves against the down comforter that only months ago touched my skin. She knows I've heard him. Silence.

"Hang on," she says, her voice almost a whisper.

Feet scuffle against bare floor. A door squeaks open, then shuts. I see her grip the phone, walk across the living room, sit on the couch, lean her head against a cushion, push her hair away from her face. It's easy to imagine. We lived together for one month, dated for five. "We are friends," I would say. "Close friends. More than friends." "You're lucky you're cute," she'd reply, "otherwise I would never let you get away with it." I miss her laugh. There is so much I can imagine. What might have happened if I'd returned home straight from the Ganges? Home, our home. Her and whatever-his-name-is's home? Maybe I don't have a home anymore. My mouth is dry.

"You okay?" Her voice again.

"I don't know."

She pauses, then lets out a long breath. "Okay. You need to know."

"Know what?" I say, my voice loud.

"Stop. Just stop. You left *me*."

Truth is a slap.

"Shit."

"You disappeared."

"I was going through stuff, I wouldn't pull you or anyone else into it."

"That's the problem, Amit."

The way she says it, her voice so sad and resigned. What an idiot I was, trying to think for her, when I didn't even know what I wanted. I want to bang my head against the glass.

"It's good you called," she says. "I need to tell you."

I shake my head. It is difficult to speak.

"You called once in three months, Amit. And that was to say you weren't coming back till whenever. I got off the phone and I was asking myself, 'What is wrong with me?' 'Why won't he come back to me?' 'Or ask me to come to him?' I would have, you know. Fool. And I asked until something inside me broke. It broke, Amit. Broke."

"Oh God," I blurt. "I'm sorry."

"I broke, Amit. I hit bottom, and it was the best thing that ever happened to me. You know why? Because I'd forgotten my own value."

She is quiet, letting that sink in. Then, her voice low.

"You are being you. It has nothing to do with me. To what I was to you. Nothing. And then I met Paul. He's good for me in a way you refused to be. I love you, but you—"

"I'm sorry."

"Listen," she says, sniffling. That's when I notice my cheeks are wet.

"I'm so sorry," I say.

"Listen."

"I'm sorry." I'm practically whining.

"Listen to me."

I stop. I just stop. "Okay."

Her voice, soft again. "Want to know the good thing about hitting bottom?"

"Please."

"There is only one way to go from there."

"A tunnel?"

She sighs. "Oh, Amit, you always were a wiseass."

I thought she liked that part of me.

"Up," she says. "You can only go up, like a Phoenix. But you have to want to."

What if I'd come home? What if I'd just called, told her everything?

"I'm a stronger and better woman. Thanks to you disappearing, I suppose."

"I aim to please." Even now, I can't help myself.

"Wiseass."

I think of something even snarkier, but nip it. We're both quiet for a long moment.

"You'll never know how much I worried," she says, softly. "All those nights."

In that moment, like a deck of cards, I see ex-girlfriends go by, flip flip flip. The ones who treated me poorly, I treated well. The ones who treated me well, like crap. Oh God. Look up "idiot" in the encyclopedia and you'll find a grinning photo of me.

"You still mean something to me and you always will."

Idiot. Idiot. Idiot. I feel like throwing up.

"I'm sorry," I say again.

"It's okay," she says. "I'm in a good place. That's all in the past."

The past. I hate the past. I blurt out the one question I don't want an answer to.

"Are you happy?"

"I'm in a good place."

Outside the booth, the breeze swirls maple leaves on the sidewalk. Dead leaves rise into the air, swirl faster and faster, then fling apart, spreading themselves across the street.

"Are you happy?" I ask again.

"Yes. Are you?"

"I don't know...sometimes when I'm hiking on these trails I feel better. Walking through countries does that, you know, takes me outside myself."

Since I don't say more, she tells me about a hurricane sliding its way through the city to upstate New York. "Ninety-mile-per-hour winds," she says. "They've even declared a state of emergency." She's a newscaster reading out headlines in the midst of a storm.

I'm craving to reach across the distance, touch her delicate fingers, her dark hair, the soft inside of her elbows, the slope of her breasts. Something inside starts to ache.

"I'm so sorry." Me, a damn broken record. "I want to explain." I take a deep breath. "I don't know what I'm doing. I just know I couldn't come back, something in me was off. And I thought, if I ran around fast enough, I would burn it away."

"Oh, Amit," she says, quiet. "I know what's wrong with you."

"I bet."

"Not that way, silly. What's wrong with you now."

Versus before? I'm sure I deserve that too.

"You hit bottom when your dad died," she says. "You just won't admit it."

She waits while I soak it in. If that was a bottom, then I've just gone deeper. Apparently, bottom has levels.

Then, thousands of miles between us, I hear her.

"Did you trust me when we were together? To be there for you no matter what? Did…you…trust…me?"

She was there when I got the call that my father wasn't expected to make it through the night. She'd held me close, gently, like I was fragile. Like if she let go, I would shatter.

"What about what's-his-name?"

"Paul?"

"Whatever."

"You didn't answer."

"It doesn't matter," I say. "People let us down. They hurt you, they run away, they leave, they die. I can't go there." I shake my head in the booth. "Not now."

There is a crack on the phone.

"Did you hear that?" she asks.

"The sound?"

"It's lightning and thunder outside. I should go soon."

I only hear muffled echoes in my head.

"Fine."

"One thing," she says. "Tell me one nice thing."

A habit of hers. If I was ever grouchy, she'd bug me for this one thing, and after finally sharing, I always felt better. Does she now do this with him? Maybe he never gets grouchy.

A yellowed leaf sticks itself to the glass, veins like an outstretched palm. I think of walking through open fields, running my hands across wheat stalks, listening to them rustle, smelling them.

"This pilgrimage," I say. "I've had moments when I just stop thinking and it feels like it's all going to be okay."

"Wow," she says. "Sounds beautiful."

"The people on this walk, they seem crazy. Bona fide. But I like them."

"I'm glad you have it," she says, her voice a whisper. "I really am. You need it."

I'm tempted to blurt out, "I need you too," but catch myself. We're both quiet for what seems like forever.

I hear a low voice. "Call me when you're coming home."

"Home?" I let out a sarcastic laugh. "My stuff's still at your place?"

"It's in storage."

"Fair enough," I say, then a deep anger rises. "Don't pay the fee. Let them throw it out. I don't care."

I catch myself. Idiot. Damn grandstanding idiot.

"I'm sorry. I don't know when that'll be."

"The fee's covered." Her voice is tight.

"Thanks."

"Bye."

Then, I'm alone.

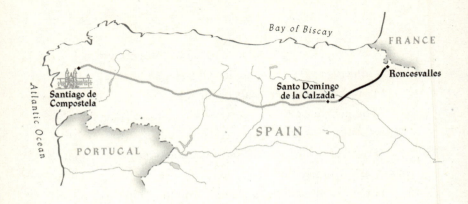

## Day Six

In the morning, once I'm sure that everyone has left, I go to the bathroom. After having been used by over thirty pilgrims, it is dirty and the floor is a mess. Wet footprints everywhere. The hot water is finished so I take a short cold shower.

Outside the refuge, flocks of crows, the bottoms of their wings dark under the sun, land on power lines, archways, rooftops. I cross a bridge at the outskirts of town and look back over the river at rows of houses, windows, lines of drying laundry. It helps to have a set direction to move toward when your mind doesn't want to think.

The rest of the day, I walk alone, mainly along a two-lane road through towns that grow larger. When I reach a small city, it takes over an hour to walk on cobblestone streets that turn into paved roads and weave past residential areas, children playing noisily in parks, outdoor stalls with fresh produce, and finally, I am at the entrance to a cathedral.

Inside, with the enormous arched pillars, the high domed ceiling, candles, and the stained glass windows streaming in wisps of blue and red and yellow light, I feel, for a moment, awe. The atmosphere makes you almost want to believe. I sit in a wooden pew, close my eyes, and rest.

"I don't want to pray to you," I say softly. "This is not a prayer."

People come and go. Echoing footsteps. Coughs.

"But if there is something out there, if you listen, just make this better. That's all I want."

In that moment, I realize I'm not asking for Sue's return. If she did, I'd still screw it up. All I want is this pain to go away.

"Please," I whisper. "Don't let me stay at bottom."

When I exit the doors and blink into the sun, the real world with its beggars and tourists outside the gates returns as a shock.

I walk to the far end of the plaza, away from the crowds, and sit on an empty bench. Behind me, a man relaxes in a folding chair against the wall. A boom box at his feet plays gentle piano music.

A group of pilgrims walk by, laughing. They are easy to identify: sunburned; wearing sandals and flip-flops after a long day's walk; pale ankles that didn't get tanned through boots and socks; some limping from blisters. The evening traffic and noise from nearby cafés grow louder.

I glance back. The man's brown hair is unkempt and there is white stubble on his face. He gently moves his hands in the air with the music.

"It's a little cold," I say. Less than a week and I can almost handle basic Spanish.

He drops his hands on his lap. "Hello."

"Warm?"

He raps the shopping cart to his left. It's loaded with blankets and sleeping bags.

"I have blankets," he says.

I walk over and shake his hand. It feels rough, callused. There are black streaks on it, like grease stains.

"The police," he says. "They let me sleep here. They know me for years and years."

I nod at the crowded plaza. "It's better here than there."

"In the day it is hot," he says, adjusting a shiny green sleeping bag over his legs, "and the night is cold. The other night, the wind was blowing hard."

He gestures at two small metal grates set in the pavement.

"I slept there," he says. "I slept there and it was warm."

I drop a few coins into an empty cup on the boom box. "Stay warm."

"God bless you," he says, smiling.

I go to a café and order a sandwich. While I'm eating, I have an idea. I buy another one, ask the waiter to wrap it, and return to the plaza.

Music echoes under the awning, piano with strings. A Tchaikovsky waltz. I feel the sharp sting of tears but shake them off. I give the man the sandwich.

He unwraps the newspaper and slowly looks up at me.

"Thank you," he says. "You are going to Santiago?"

"Yes," I lie. No need getting into specifics.

"Where is your home?"

"I am from New York."

He bites into the sandwich. "So," he says, chewing. "How are you?"

"Sick," I say. "Trying to get better."

"That is everyone's story."

I turn to go. "Keep warm."

He raises a hand, palm up. "Goodbye, pilgrim from New York."

Past his hand, I see the two metal grates. I walk away, still feeling sick. But just slightly less so.

Instead of going to the local refuge, I spend the night in a *pensión*. It's just an extra room in an upstairs apartment with a balcony that looks out over the spires of the cathedral. It puts a dent in my budget, but I don't care. One more day, then no more pilgrims and their snoring.

I help myself to a bottle of scotch in the kitchen, pouring it into the tallest glass available, then sit in the balcony. Straight liquor reminds me of my father, the smell, the anger. But right now, I just don't care. The faster I'm numb, the better. I take a long sip and swirl the scotch around my mouth before swallowing. My lips tingle.

What an ass I've been. All this time, wandering, and Sue, crying by herself, hitting bottom. Because of me. She's better off without me. I go round and round, beating myself up, and when I really can't stand myself anymore, I remember the Frenchwoman, the way she laughed at me.

Nothing to lose, I kiss the back of my hand. Then I kiss it again. The third time, like I mean it. I'm not exactly jumping for joy, but it shifts me. She might have been on to something.

"Okay," I say out loud. "If I loved myself, what would I do?"

The monk from Dharamsala flashes by. His smile.

"Say yes."

"Hey," I say, then laugh slightly. "To what, this?"

"Say yes."

"*If* I loved myself...?"

"Say yes."

No place to return to, no more girlfriend, wanting to run away from the sight of a hospital, from all that death. Which obviously throws my becoming a doctor out the window. Imagine that med school interview.

I stir the ice in the glass with my little finger. The spires of the cathedral are dark shadows in the night. I could travel somewhere else, sit on a beach, and drink until my money ran out. Or go home.

"Home," I say out loud, with exaggerated air quotes.

Go home, buy a gun, find Sue, and off myself in front of her.

"Wouldn't that be fun?" I say. "A blast."

He stands silent, holding his hand out palm up, beads in the other.

"No yes, huh?" I mock him. I mock an actual monk.

I drink in large sips. Whatever I'm burning through my system slowly lessens.

"Say yes." He smiles.

"Easy for you," I mumble. "You left everything behind."

Then I realize, I've sort of done the same myself.

"Say yes."

I stare at the back of my hand.

"I'll think about it."

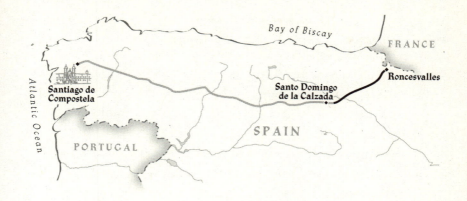

# Day Seven

Glasses in hand, Loïc and I sit on the steps outside the refuge. Birds chirp loudly. Underbellies of clouds glow violet under the setting sun. I sip the whiskey. As the Camino's progressing, more and more refuges have bars next door. Coincidence?

"Hey Loïc," I say, clinking glasses. "I thought the French only liked wine."

"Well, we like many things."

"What do the French like besides wine?"

He grins slowly. "Ladies."

No matter my mood, I love this guy.

"I mean, in a glass."

"Oh yes, we like whiskey very much. But unfortunately, that is English."

I chuckle, remembering that he told me the French agreed to the Chunnel so they could finally civilize the English. We return to the sunset. Children kick a soccer ball across the street, pausing whenever a car drives by. They shout at each other and run back and forth, their arms flailing. By the time our glasses are almost empty, I need to get it off my chest.

"I spoke with a friend yesterday," I say. "She thinks that I've hit bottom."

He turns, face furrowing into concern. I grab his wrist. He watches me, his eyes sharp, then pats my forearm.

"*Oui*. I will not push."

I drop his wrist. "Sorry."

"It's nothing, *mon ami*." A long pause. "May I share?"

I shrug: Go for it.

"*Félicitations*." He actually reaches over, pumps my hand hard. "Congratulations."

If I had any whiskey in my mouth, I would have spit it out in surprise.

"I have known a few great men and women in my life," he says. "All, without exception, became great after, as you say, they hit bottom. It is as if, for the first time in life, they had to discover who they were. What they were made of."

He's quiet for a long moment.

"Book of Job," he says finally. "The thing I feared most came upon me."

"Good thing you're not religious."

He laughs. "Yes. Then I would be dangerous."

I give him an imaginary toast.

"One more thing," he says. "I experienced my own fall. What it was, that does not matter in this moment. But I...I rose from the ashes."

Ashes. Bottom. Phoenix. Sue.

"I removed what was not me. I became the real me. It is perhaps the best thing that happened in my life."

He stands, clasps my shoulder.

"But I am far from a great man."

I hold his hand. "You're not so bad."

He grins, then leaves for his hotel. The evening slides into a dark blue. The whiskey's kicked in rather nice and it feels good to be alone, quiet. The only problem: the more you want it, the more people interrupt you. Two pilgrims come and sit by my side.

One's a German architect from the Black Forest. Nice enough guy. The other, Nick, a Scottish pilgrim about my age, I could care less about. I met him at a previous refuge and made the mistake of calling him "English." Fun lecture on Scottish history that night.

That led to a discussion of bagpipes, which he told me he played, and I told him sounded like a sheep being beaten to death. Dear friends, I can say, we're not.

While they chatter away, I sip the remaining whiskey and tune them out.

"I forgot to ask you," the German says to me. "What did you think of Ignacio?"

"Who?"

"Aye," Nick says. "The crazy painter."

"The what?"

"Ignacio," the German says, shifting closer. "You mean you missed him?"

I feel trapped. Nick stretches out his long legs, crosses and uncrosses them. I wish he would stop moving.

"Oh," Nick says. "You'll hate yourself for this."

Then they start talking, more between each other than to me. From what I can make out, earlier this afternoon, they passed a sign pointing to a building. It was clearly designed for pilgrims. So they followed it and a wild-looking man came out, took them in, and poured them wine in golden goblets.

With a pang, I remember the sign with the image of a scallop shell. It was nailed to a tree, and when I passed it, I was too busy feeling sorry for myself to pay attention.

"We were drunk with wine," the German says, tapping my arm to make sure I'm listening. "Then he asked us to close our eyes. He was a good man. I trusted him. He put a cross around our necks. He had carved them himself."

Nick clasps his neck with both hands. "He pulled the string as if he was choking me, but I heard him laughing, crazy wanker, and when I opened my eyes, I saw the cross."

"He was a generous man," the German says. "He would not let us give anything in return. His crosses are famous on the Camino."

Keeping up with them is making me dizzy. I try to stand but notice Nick digging a cross out of his pocket. I sit down. The cross is thick, about the size of my hand, and carved from dark oak. The architect pulls his out. Each is unique and follows the natural curves of the wood.

Nick starts rattling on again. When the German joins in, I figure out the rest. Ignacio gave them a tour of his studio. It was full of sculptures made from metal, wood, mirrors. He even had an original Picasso hanging in the mess.

"Everyone met him." Nick gestures to the refuge behind us. "Go on, ask them. It's a pity you missed out."

He puts the cross away. I just want this day to be over.

Dinner is served in a small room in the basement of the bar. Pilgrims sit at a long table, talking loudly and laughing. Wooden crosses hang from their necks. Except mine. I stay quiet, moving the food around my plate with a fork. Mostly, I drink wine, and when I can't stand it anymore, I grab a glass and bottle and go out into the cool, night air.

The bar's parking lot is empty. I sit against a wall on the asphalt, and quickly drink a glass to warm myself up. Lights in the village go out one by one. I feel like a lone traveler in the desert. He knows that there's much out there: oases, palm trees, travelers seeking shelter, camels needing water. But when he gazes at the sky above, the sand dunes ahead, he only sees emptiness.

The door opens. A woman's voice, laughter, the door shuts. Footsteps. Roseangela.

"You are all right?" she asks.

The way she says it causes tears to form at the backs of my eyes. I blink and nod, looking away. She brushes the area next to me with her hand and sits down. Our shoulders touch and I feel her warmth. God, it feels so good.

"You have been quiet," she says.

"I'm okay."

"Very American," she says, empty glass on her knees. " 'I'm okay.' Very polite, means nothing."

I fill her glass, refill mine. We clink and drink in silence. High beyond the rooftops of the village, the Milky Way is a bright haze.

"I called my girlfriend."

"Oh, how nice."

"She's an ex-girlfriend now."

"Oh." A pause. "I am sorry."

"It happens." This woman's got her own cross to bear. No need adding to its weight.

Through the darkness, I can feel her watching me.

"You do not like to talk about many things," she says quietly.

"I didn't mean it that way," I say, take a sip. "Even when I was in India, my aunt wanted me to talk about my fa—" I stop. "Anyway. But why talk? All it does is bring up memories."

"You will talk," she says. "When the time is right. When you need it."

I shift, face her. "It's been about four months since I left home," I say, "and now, I don't know what I have to return to."

She leans back on her hands, gazes at the sky.

"When I was in the Himalayas," I say, "the things I saw. Jagged peaks of fluorescent white. I've never seen anything like it. I mean, when the sun shone, those mountains glowed. They were so bright. They—"

She touches my wrist gently. "I understand."

"Anyway. They've been here long before us and they'll be around long after." I nod at the night sky. "Just like those stars."

I take a long sip.

"I'll bet they laugh at us. How personally we take everything."

She smiles softly. Even the corners of her eyes smile.

"What?"

She shakes her head, continues smiling. Something in my chest starts to warm. I refill our glasses.

She lets out a giggle. "I am a little drunk."

"Join the club."

She sits forward, pulls her jacket over her knees.

"You are on the Camino. You are a pilgrim." She glances at the bar. "We are all pilgrims."

"My situation's different," I say. "This wasn't some grand life goal of mine. I just sort of showed up."

She shakes her head, smiling.

"Accidental pilgrim," she says slowly, "is still a pilgrim."

The night is bright enough for me to make out her face. Her eyelashes are long and curved.

"There." Roseangela points up. "There!"

I look up. Stars everywhere. No moon.

"What?"

She makes an arcing motion with her hand.

"Shooting star?"

"Yes. Very beautiful."

We see several shooting stars and each time we point them out, she laughs. I show her a tiny, white dot moving slowly past the heavens.

"A satellite."

"Humans can create stars," she says, clapping her hands. Pure delight.

The way she says it, I have a sudden urge to kiss her. I take a swig straight from the bottle instead. My limbs are tingly and numb to the cold.

"What was Ignacio like?"

"Wonderful," she says. "Very special."

"I'm angry at myself for missing out." I point to her cross. "On that."

She giggles, covers her mouth, and breaks out into laughter.

"What's so funny?"

"You are," she manages to say, then starts laughing again. "You are so serious," she says when she finally stops. Her voice rises. "I should be in my mother's house, crying, but I am here. Why? Because to walk the Camino is my dream. I choose to be here. We hold ourselves back, not life."

*If* I loved myself...

"Life says move forward. Like the Camino."

What would I do?

"It reminds me of something," I say, and tell her about Loïc's theory on the heart versus reason. Of magic. I tell her about the monk. She smiles and pushes on my shoulder for leverage as she stands.

"I think," she says, steadying herself. "I think that you made your decision."

"What decision?"

"You know."

She bends down for her glass. The dolphins hang past her cheeks and I start to reach out, touch her face, feel her warmth, but catch myself. She notices my eyes.

"This," she says, removing Ignacio's cross from her neck. "For you."

I start to protest but a finger on my lips stops me.

"Oh, my serious pilgrim," she says in that singsong voice of hers. "Lower your head."

I do as she asks. She puts the string over my head and tugs. Her voice, gentle. "You need this more than me."

Cross against my sternum, I look up at her. She smiles a slow, delicious smile and runs a finger across my cheek. The touch, so soft. My heart thumps in my ears. Then she straightens and walks toward the refuge.

*"Boa noite."* Her voice blends into the night.

I stare at the cross on my chest for a long time.

*If* I loved myself, I would...

I finally say it. To the monk. To the Camino. To whoever is pulling the damn strings.

"Yes."

# Day Nine

Dawn appears, a dark shade of red mixed with orange, like a colorful sari at an Indian wedding. Pilgrims head west. I find a phone booth and make another call.

"Mom."

Across the Atlantic, the pleasure in her voice.

"Hello, *beta*."

"I'm a pilgrim."

A pause. Then laughter.

"Well, your aunt would enjoy that."

Despite her worrying, she does get me. Maybe that's why we've only fought twice in my life. And when I say "we," I mean me.

The first time, over a man. After we left my father, there were a few, and each I liked less and less, until one day in high school, Bob or Schmob or whatever his name was, cut her off at dinner. I grabbed his plate, threw his food in the trash, and sat down across from him, glaring. He left shortly after, and she cried and said nothing. No more men came around.

The second time, last year, when she admitted that she'd been taking care of my father after chemotherapy rounds. I actually yelled at her to stop. She was silent on the phone, letting me go on, then finally, her voice quiet and firm, "He's a dying man, *beta*. Let it go."

Her, of all people, what she went through. It floored me. I hung up, unable to talk. My hands were trembling.

"When will you be ready to come home?"

"I honestly don't know, Mom."

"Do you need money?"

"No." This, I need to do on my own.

I tell her about the Camino. She listens without interrupting once.

"I wish I had done something like it," she says.

I'd told Sue a bit about our life, how hard she worked. Minimum-wage jobs, cleaning houses, whatever paid. That time after we left my father, us standing at a train station, two suitcases, no place to go, my mother holding my hand and silently crying.

"You're a strong woman," Sue said to her the first time they met.

"No," my mother said. "My child. I looked at him. That gave me strength."

I often feel guilt over the happiness she sacrificed for me. I almost tell her about Sue, but nip the idea. No need adding to her worries. She thought Sue was good for me.

"Call me soon," she says. "And be safe."

"I will, Mom."

"And listen to me," she says. "I know this has been hard on you. Do what you need to do, okay? I know you can take care of yourself, but I worry."

"I know, Mom."

"And, *beta*?"

"Yes, Mom?"

"Let it go. Just let it go, *beta*."

I take a breath and say it for her.

"I'll try, Mom. I promise."

After we're done, I pop a few painkillers to dull the ache in my shoulders and wash them down. Ahead, golden wheat fields roll and stretch into the horizon. I walk into them.

# Day Eleven

"Did you see the Englishman crying loudly in his bed?" Nick asks.

"No." I continue reading the guidebook.

"But he was right there."

I turn the page. "Didn't see him."

We sit at a crowded kitchen table in a refuge in Santo Domingo de la Calzada. Outside, buses pull into the plaza. Tourists holding cameras step out and mingle with tired, sunburned pilgrims. Dusk is approaching and the cobblestones in the plaza are a dull gray.

I miss Roseangela. Several days ago, while I slowed down because of a tweaked ankle, courtesy of a rather spectacular fall in a muddy field, she increased her pace.

"My heart, it is telling me to move faster," she said.

A problem with the Camino: fall one refuge ahead or

behind someone, and you might never see them again. With each day, the prospect of drifting farther apart compounds.

I grip my ankle, press against it with both thumbs. The pain is almost gone. Odds or not, I can pick up my pace again, try to catch up with Roseangela. The check-in ledger here showed that she passed through a day ago. Just as I'm working out my new schedule, there's a loud thud. The sound of a body hitting something hard.

A man's voice, muffled behind the closed door. "I'm fine. I'm fine." Then, cackling laughter.

The door flies open, bangs against the wall. Nick's face hangs open. Suddenly, a man jumps through the doorway and into the crowded kitchen.

"Ha!" the skinny man shouts, glaring at silent pilgrims. He stomps in, boots making a loud clomp clomp, fists on his hips. "Ha!"

The man's face is red. Not sunburned like the rest of us, just bright red. His beard is a scraggly white, his hair is wind-blown, and his eyes are bloodshot. He wobbles, then leans back on his heels. He grins.

"That's him," Nick whispers excitedly. "Him! The crying Englishman."

"I'm Ron." He grabs the nearest woman's hand. "A plea-sure." He kisses it sloppily several times.

"Lovely start, eh?"

Silence.

"Ready?"

"For what?" the woman asks.

He gently guides her to a crowded table, moving pilgrims aside to make room.

"You'll have a better view here, luv," he says, winking slyly.

Then, he starts singing the cowboy western song, "The Ballad of High Noon." He stamps his feet, he blows kisses at women, he dances around the tables. The wooden floor shakes. I imagine paint chips raining from the ceiling below. I have to admit, I'm enjoying the looks on everyone's faces.

Once finished, he bows, and we clap. While he's busy shaking every hand he can, I notice that it's already dark through the windows, and walk out.

Lampposts throw long shadows on the sidewalk. A woman passes me, her heels clicking loudly on the cobblestones. I reach a street lined with shops, the steel shutters down and locked, and stop at a pay phone at the corner.

I dial the number for home. My stomach feels queasy. Ex-home. That doesn't make it any better. The phone rings and then voicemail.

"I can't take your call right now..."

She changed the message. I hang up.

What was I hoping for? Maybe what's-his-name is history and she'll wait for me. But what if she said only if I returned right away? I'm not ready. What if she's avoiding me? What if he's with her? I try one more time.

"Answer," I whisper, the plastic hard against my ear. Seconds pass. "Please."

Straight to voicemail. I slam the receiver and return to the refuge.

The dark kitchen smells of tomatoes and garlic. I light a candle on the table and help myself to the leftover spaghetti. Fortunately, there are plenty of half-finished wine bottles as well. I work on emptying them.

After a while, I hear a cough, then Ron joins me.

"All right?" he asks.

I can see the veins in his eyes, cracks of red.

"Sure."

I fill a glass, slide it over.

"Ah yes." He licks his lips. "Much better. Much better."

He drains the wine, lets me refill it.

"Old wankers." He flicks a thumb at the bunkroom. "All asleep."

Agewise, he must be the oldest pilgrim in the refuge. By far.

"People," he says, disgust in his voice, "they don't live. You go off for five years and see the world and you return, they're still the same. Driving to work"—he makes a robotic gesture, stiff arms around an imaginary steering wheel—"drinking their tea. You know what it says to me? They're waiting to die. Bleeding bores. Life is short. We've got to take it, live it."

He slaps the back of his neck, rubs something off his hand.

"Past summer, I spent two weeks in the Amazon traveling from village to village in a canoe. The natives, they've got it right."

He grows quiet and turns away. Moments pass.

Softly, he says, "I know where I am going when I die."

I skip the obvious question. Right now, I couldn't care less where drunk Englishmen end up. Probably France.

He rummages through his pockets and pulls out a black-and-white feather. He rubs it along his cheek, sniffs.

"It's very special to me, the Camino. This is my second time. I'm no rocket scientist, but I know what's right and this"—he waves a hand—"this is right." He puts the feather in my palm. "You mind?"

"No," I say, the feather soft and tickling.

"The Camino." His face quivers. "It's been very good to me. The feather, it's from an eagle, you see. I found it. I walked out of this refuge one morning and there it was at my feet, waiting. I know my grandson is here, I know it."

Something inside me goes "uh-oh."

"Are you alone here?" he asks.

I nod yes.

"Me too, this time." He points to his face, the arcing lines around the sides of his mouth. They are visible through the thinning beard. "Some are from laughter, but not all, mind you. Not all."

"Why alone this time?"

"To chase away ghosts," he says, voice tight, strained. "And to say goodbye." He grabs my arm tightly, his voice lowers. "I am an emotional man. I like being emotional, especially when I have a drink."

He lets go, pulls out a yellow lion-shaped pipe from a velvety purple pouch. The lion's mouth is open, as if in the middle of a roar. He adds the tobacco, lights it with a match, and puffs slowly, the sweet tobacco smell filling the kitchen.

"I meet people on the Camino," he says. "All sorts of remarkable people, and I laugh and I cry with them. I shed my tears."

His gray eyes focus past me, staring far, far away.

"My grandson died four months ago," he says quietly.

Darkness enters through the window, etches deep wrinkles on his face. The candle flickers. He closes his eyes, suddenly looking very old and very tired.

"Sixteen." His voice is barely a whisper. "Just a boy. I never even got to say goodbye."

"I'm so sorry."

He pats my arm. Tears form at the corners of his eyes, follow the grooves of the wrinkles, lose themselves in the beard. I pass him a napkin. He shakes his head.

"I miss him. Oh, I miss him. When I cry, I think I'll lose myself. But the tears, they can't wash the missing away."

Standing by the river. The charcoal-like dust. No going back, no redoing of things that were done, no fixing mistakes that were made. I wanted to fling the box into the water, walk away. "You've caused me enough pain," I wanted to scream. "I will not cry for you." My eyes had throbbed but I'd stopped the tears.

"Do they help?"

"Wine helps. I drink a bottle every night." He manages a slight smile. "Sometimes more."

I take that as a cue and try to fill his glass, but he pushes the bottle away.

"No, it's good to think about him right now."

"Memories are hard."

"They're all I've got left." He grabs the napkin from my hand and wipes his face. He blows his nose. "I am an emotional man."

"That's okay."

He clears his throat. "I can't sleep," he says, "not unless I drink. That's why I'm here. The boy loved the countryside, you see. He would understand this. In Santiago, I will say goodbye."

Is that what I'm doing, too, without realizing it, walking to say goodbye? I hope not. One goodbye at the Ganges was enough.

"We do have our pain," he says. "And joys. Never forget

that. He is with me, you know. I can feel him when I'm out there and I talk to him. I know that he hears me."

The pipe dies. He cleans it and returns it to the pouch.

"Hey," I say. "Did you meet Ignacio, the crazy artist?"

He shakes his head. "No. But I rather like the description."

I smile. "Hang on a moment."

I run to the bunkroom and return with the cross. I hand it to him. He turns it around, admires it.

"What's this?"

"From the crazy artist. A gift."

He rubs his thumbs along the grain. "It's stunning," he says and tries to hand it back.

"This is yours," I say. "You need it more than me."

We stare at each other for a moment.

"Oh," he says. He bends forward, pulls the string over his thinning hair, and straightens. The cross hangs next to his heart. "Oh," he says, voice very quiet. "I am a sentimental man."

It's way late. If I'm going to walk long days to catch up with Roseangela, I better rest.

"I'm hitting the sack," I say.

He nods. "Tell you what, the feather. Keep it."

"Ron, I can't—"

"No, no. Keep it, please. A gift from my grandson. To you. I reckon you're chasing ghosts as well."

I just want to hug this guy. So I do. Long and tight.

"Two partners," he whispers into my ear. His voice is hoarse. "Fear and faith. The one you dance with determines your life."

Finished, he slaps my shoulder.

"Go on. Don't look back, because that's when it hurts."

# Day Thirteen

The bar is warm and crowded. Pilgrims walk in, stamp their feet, rub their hands, buy a drink, and head for the fireplace. This stretch of the Camino, the Montes de Oca, is known for its harsh, unpredictable weather and steep hills covered with pine forests. Easy place to get lost and disappear. Bandits used to hide here, rob and kill passing pilgrims, but in the twelfth century, a monk named Juan cleared a path through the hills and helped build roads, bridges, and hospitals. After his death, he somehow developed a reputation for curing sterility, his monastery serving pilgrims and, at one time, doubling as a medieval fertility clinic. Today the monastery still stands, along with this bar, and a priest famous for his garlic soup.

In the evening, we go to the church. Even though this is a pilgrimage, many pilgrims, including myself, don't regularly attend mass. But here, everyone wants to see the priest who makes the garlic soup.

The inside of the church is lit by rows of tall candles. The tomb of Saint Juan rests in the middle of the pews and is protected by spiked bars. Short and stocky with a head of white hair, the priest greets us, then stands by the altar.

"Each of you is searching," he says. "You are letting the road guide you. That is the power of the Camino. It does not matter why you are here or that you get to Santiago. It's what you learn that is important."

On the walk to Pamplona, Roseangela had told me something similar. She passed through a day ago. I miss the way her dolphin earrings shook when she laughed.

The priest gives out communion. Even from the pew, I can see his eyes shine. I want to talk with him, find out his secret, but know it already: he's living his purpose. I join the long line and, for the first time on the Camino, eat the wafer and drink from the cup like the pilgrims who came before me. The priest nods at me and smiles, making me feel welcome. It's a beautiful feeling.

After service, the famous garlic soup is served in a hall on the ground floor of the monastery. The place is packed with pilgrims, many that I'm starting to recognize. But most important, Loïc is here. I missed him, too. Through the open doorway, we can see the priest talking loudly and laughing in the kitchen.

He finally comes out with two men carrying a large red pot. They set it down on a table and pass the soup out in bowls. The priest chats and watches us eat.

"We are Germans, Spanish, Italian, French, English, Americans," a pilgrim says loudly. "Here together. Can you imagine that in my grandfather's day, we were killing each other?"

We're quiet for a solemn moment, looking at each other, and all of a sudden, as if on cue, we break into smiles. Respect for the past, but leave it behind in the intimacy of this simple shared experience. We return to our food.

It feels good to hold the bowl, sip slowly, and feel the steam warm my face. I waited all day for this. The soup itself isn't much more than hot broth, but the company and the laughter spice it to perfection.

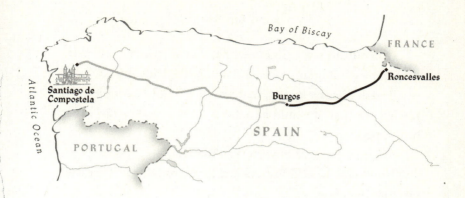

## Day Fourteen

"They're not soft. Not like I thought they'd be."

"Yes?"

"When you open the box and dump them into the river, the wind, it blows them back at you."

Behind us, hills covered in pines. Ahead, golden brown wheat as far as the eye can see. Clouds drift overhead, their shadows dark and massive patches on the fields below.

"I mean, there you are, standing with the ashes of a dead man, your father, all over your clothes, your skin."

My voice grows louder. I can't help it.

"You're practically inhaling him."

Hand on my shoulder, gentle. *"Mon ami."*

"And the worst part, the worst part, how're you supposed to react? Return home, back to real life, pretend everything's all right? But inside you've got these things you know you should have done, shouldn't have done...and now it's too late."

The trail rises in a slight incline, then dips and rises again. I stop, the wind on my face, and watch the fields shift.

"I wish I hadn't known that he was dying," I say quietly. "I really wish that. It would have been so much easier not to see him suffer."

"It is never easy. Not with such matters."

"You know what?" I say, facing away from him. "It's easier not to think about it."

"And sometimes," I hear him say, "it is no good to remain with a cold head. Sometimes it is purely a matter of the heart."

I slowly face him. He looks at me with gentle, brown eyes.

"I am very much moved by what you said." He pats my arm. "This I can advise you: all that has happened, the death of your father, your travel to India, the questioning of your profession, the Camino, it is part of the same road. It is connected. You may not realize this now, but after time, you will see that there was a reason."

Here I am with money running out, still no idea what I want to do, no girlfriend.

"You will see." He flashes his trademark grin. "I can assure you."

We resume walking and are quiet. He hums to himself, and whenever our eyes meet, we smile.

"Want to know something?" I ask after a while.

"Yes. Of course."

"When I went away, I was living paycheck to paycheck. My father had wired money to my aunt for me, before he died. I found out about it after I got to India. Because of that, I can afford this."

"A final gift," he says, "to do what you must."

"He didn't know me, Loïc."

"He knew. A father knows."

I watch him for a moment. He has a daughter close to my age, a son five years older.

"Loïc?"

"Yes?"

"The experience of having children...I mean, is it worth it?"

"Experience? I can assure you, having a child, it is not an experience. It is a way of life. I have never for a moment regretted it. I have often wondered about men like Eiffel. He built many bridges in France, and, of course, the Eiffel Tower. The man, he is gone, but his work remains." He shakes his head. "Your work is an important matter, yes, but your children, they carry on a part of you, and in ways you can never predict or expect."

A strap on his daypack is loose and I can hear the plastic end hit the water bottle with each step. I think of the last time I saw my father in the hospital: his eyes moving, his body a bruised, brown skeleton. The ventilator made a squishing sound as it pushed air into his lungs. Air in, squish, pause, air out, squish, pause, air in. The room had an antiseptic hospital smell. A medical student, obvious by the short lab coat, walked in to draw his blood. I wanted to grab him by his white coat, fling him across the waxed floor. "There's nothing left," I wanted to shout. "Get your practice somewhere else." Instead, I stood in silence. The medical student looked at me, lowered his eyes, unhooked the IV from the arm, clipped the glass tube to the needle. It filled with a dark, red liquid. Heart still pumped, eyes still searched.

Wind blows across the fields, bending the stalks in ripples, like waves coming to shore. The wind grows louder, the waves rougher. I'm alone, drinking every night. What else am I carrying of my father?

The trail curves to the left, leads to a village, and ends at a bar. Loïc holds the door open and we go in, eyes adjusting to the darkness. A woman stands behind the counter, washing glasses. Tight dress, straight dark hair down to her shoulders.

Loïc glances at her, then the bottles arranged above the counter. He rubs his hands.

"Ah, civilization."

Two pilgrims are playing a pinball machine near the door.

"Her eyes." Loïc leans in close and whispers. "So mysterious, so beautiful. She should be in a city. What is she doing here?"

I shrug. At least outside, with the cool air and smell of fields, it was easier to lose myself. But now, in the darkness, I can feel the throbbing behind my eyes. It's difficult to concentrate.

"Oh yes, I know," Loïc continues. "She is waiting for us."

He walks to the counter. The pinball machine is loud and the flashing lights make my headache worse. I go to the bathroom, shut the door, wash my hands, splash water on my face. I look at my reflection in the smudged mirror above the sink. My eyes are red. I lean back against the wall, close my eyes, and try to breathe slowly, but through the darkness, through the splotches of color as I squeeze my eyes tight, the past returns.

A young boy heads home with his mother. It is evening and the birds are chirping. He is skipping instead of walking and his mother is laughing. They enter their apartment and go to the kitchen. The light is on. The boy sees his father sitting at the table, his right hand holding a glass half filled with a yellow, silky liquid. There are two empty bottles on the table. A moth slowly circles around the bulb in the ceiling, its shadow fluttering on the walls.

The boy can feel his mother standing next to him. Everything is quiet. He looks up and sees the moth go round and round. The room feels hot and his mouth tastes metallic. He lowers his gaze and sees that his father's thin lips are closed and he is breathing through his nose. His eyes are bloodshot and he is clenching the glass tighter, threatening to explode the world into shards.

The boy grabs his mother's hand, squeezes it, and feels the fear seep through her skin until it becomes his own.

My eyes had started a few days earlier: a slight pinkishness. I stopped at a pharmacy, bought the medicine the woman recommended, but they continued getting redder. My rational mind reminded me that infections happen sometimes. But at night, when I lay awake in the darkness, I saw flames rushing through the land, consuming everything in their path, and leaving behind ash, which floated slowly, like a gentle snowfall.

I open my eyes and squint at the mirror. Still red. When I return, Loïc is leaning on the counter and chatting with the woman.

"You appear tired," he says to me.

"I'm just hungry."

A ham leg hangs from the wooden beam above. Loïc has the woman slice several pieces and orders a bottle of Rioja. We eat the salty, dry ham and drink the cold wine.

Loïc leans close. "Spanish girls, yes, they are very pretty. Some nights I still cannot sleep when I think of Spanish girls I have seen twenty-five years ago. But they don't like to be touched, they are like this."

He holds his nose up in the air, making me laugh.

"You can only look." He shakes his head sadly. "I do not know how they procreate."

After lunch, the woman comes to the door and waves to Loïc as we walk single-file through the grass. The wine seems to have done my head good. I can't feel my eyes throb. We cross the highway, and then the trail widens and leads through a grassy plain. There are furrowed hills to our right.

"I will tell you of my dream from last night," Loïc says. "A wonderful dream I will never forget: my boat, sailing across the sands of the Sahara, full sail, a big, round moon."

He is quiet, as if savoring the dream.

"You know, I was once offered to crew for Rothschild, as a navigator. He wanted to race his boat—well, I will call it that but it was rather large—he wanted to race it across the Pacific, but I did not do it." His sailor eyes crinkle, as if watching something far over the horizon. "I would like to say that I never pursued it."

I shrug, not sure where he's going.

"If I tell you the truth, you will not believe it. I am afraid of the sea."

I stare at him, expecting a laugh, a lead-up to a joke. One look at his face and I know I'm wrong.

"My father was also afraid of the sea," he says. "He was actually terrified of it."

On the bus ride from Barcelona, he had told me about his family, all generations of fishermen from Brittany, a region where all the villages have chapels to honor men lost at sea.

"But when one gains a belief as a child," he says, "it is difficult to let go."

He coughs, runs a hand through his short, curly hair.

"Would you like to know when I am most alive?"

"Sure," I say.

"When I am sailing my boat. When I face my fear of the sea. My cliff, it is where I jump and grow wings."

"Your place of magic, huh?"

He grins. "Yes. Where you face your deepest fears, magic."

An arrow leads us to a two-lane road, which winds past deserted parking lots, car dealerships with chain-link fences, and then shopping centers. The sidewalk is cracked and it hurts to walk on cement. We're both quiet, a common habit on the Camino when you leave forests and wide-open fields for crowded cities.

The road adds several lanes. We pass rows of closely bunched apartment buildings with drying laundry fluttering from balconies. We smell city smells and the air grows hot and oppressive. The sidewalks are jammed with tables of outdoor cafés.

The road joins a four-way intersection and the traffic becomes gridlocked. Just as the honking and crowds grow unbearable, we enter the old section of the city of Burgos. Cobblestone roads and ancient buildings and churches appear. The traffic thins. There are statues and fountains in plazas, shady trees border both sides of the road, and a river comes into view. Loïc looks at me, and nods. We both feel the change.

At his hotel, he places his hands on my shoulders, pecks me on both cheeks.

"Your father, he had his journey. This is yours."

I blink away tears and hug him. We'll meet tomorrow night at the next refuge. I leave him at the check-in desk and follow the arrows painted on street signs. Alone again, straps digging into my neck and shoulders with each step.

Times like this, I wish I had my act together, some real change in my pocket so I could stay in a nice hotel if I wanted. Then again, if I had enough cash to do whatever I wanted, I probably wouldn't have ended up on this journey. Economy of restraints, it can lead to things.

I walk for a long while, then stop at the river to watch the flowing water. The banks are lined with trees with short white trunks and branches that reach into the sky like cupped hands.

Outside the Gothic cathedral, I see the strangest sight on the Camino: a group of Hare Krishnas dancing and singing in the plaza. As I sit on the steps and watch, one of them tries to talk to me. From his accented Spanish, it's obvious that he's American.

"You know," I say, "you might not be in the best place for this."

"Excuse me?"

"The Inquisition. The Spanish Inquisition. You've heard of it?"

"Yes."

"They named it after this country for a reason."

The joke falls flat. He doesn't laugh. "What are you doing here?"

"I'm on a pilgrimage," I say.

"You are searching for Spirit, then?"

"Yellow arrows."

I leave the plaza and instead of sticking with the boulevard, wander down side streets, passing souvenir stores, clothing shops, restaurants, bars. Outside a leather shop, I stare at jackets in a display case lit by rows of bulbs in the ceiling. The idea of wearing a leather jacket feels strange. My life has come down to what I can carry in my pack, only what is necessary. Even an extra T-shirt, after a hundred miles, makes you feel its weight. Just like memories.

# Day Fifteen

On a Sunday, in the north of Spain, I walk into the land of death.

In Pamplona, Roseangela told me that the Camino was divided into three parts: Roncesvalles to Burgos was "Life"; Burgos to León was "Death"; León to Santiago was "Rebirth."

In the land of Life, you walked through fields, vineyards, and green hills. Then you ended up in the high plains, the land of Death. No shade, no escape from the sun in the summers, freezing winters. From there, you made your way up the mountains and down into the land of Rebirth. Lush forests and gentle hills all the way to Santiago de Compostela.

I leave Burgos behind and head down the rocky trail into a valley. The hills are bare except for an occasional field. I hear the lonely sound of a cricket. Purple orchids, poppies, dandelions, and thorny bushes line the path.

Many pilgrims chose to skip this part and took the train

from Burgos to León. Some didn't want to deal with the grueling terrain, while others did it out of superstition. I'd considered joining them, the concept of death something I didn't want to explore anymore, but Loïc warned me against following the herd. "Death," he said, "has its own lessons to teach."

I pause, look behind me: blue skies. Ahead, gray. A cold wind is blowing. I zip up my fleece jacket and continue down the steep descent known as the Cuesta de Matamulos, Mule Killer Hill. The footprints of those who went before me stand out in the dry, cracked earth.

As I grow closer to a village at the edge of the valley, the bushes grow taller, some almost four to five feet high, with leaves shaped like spikes. A small lark sits on a bush and watches me pass by. It is the shade of dead grass. There is the sound of running water, then the path crosses a stream. I turn back once more and see a curving brown trail rising into the hills. The bird chirps louder and louder until I walk away.

The church tower in the village has two openings on top for giant bells, like black, hollow eyes. Watching. Not judging or expecting, simply watching. I cross a stone bridge at the outskirts and the sun streams through the clouds. When I look up, it is like a pinhole in the sky.

The main street is lined with houses with caved-in roofs, missing doors and windows. I pass one with rows of hanging beads for a door. The beads run against each other in the breeze.

The refuge is next to the church and, behind it, a small cemetery. I claim bunks for Loïc and myself by spreading my things over them.

Two pilgrims in their early twenties who passed me earlier today are in the courtyard of the church. An older pilgrim sits in a corner, writing in a notebook. One of the young pilgrims is from Iceland, the other from France. The Icelander is tall and has pale, almost-white eyebrows and hair, while the Frenchman has a scraggly beard and smells like he hasn't showered lately. They boast that they average fifty kilometers a day. Many pilgrims, including myself, walk somewhere around twenty.

"Are you training for the Camino Olympics?" I ask.

They shrug, pop open cans of beer, take deep swallows, say that they want to show me something, and lead me to the cemetery. What I see leaves me speechless. A few gravestones and markers are intact, while the rest lie broken, or lean as if about to fall any minute. The ground is littered with human bones. Femurs, vertebrae, humors, tibias, fibulas, ribs, partial and whole skulls stick up through the grass and mud. Others lie in odd positions, as if having been thrown around.

The two take a skull, prop it on a gravestone, and wedge beer cans on both sides like ears. Then they squat alongside and take photos.

"This is what happens when you drink too much," the Icelander says, making the French pilgrim laugh. He pops open another can.

The skull is a question mark against the gray sky. I look away. From where I stand, I can see the valley I entered today. I hear the two laugh, watch them spray each other with beer, and throw bones around until I can't take it any longer.

"Don't you have any respect?"

That makes them giggle. As the Frenchman moves to spray me with beer, I step forward, grab the can in his hand, hold it tight.

"Don't," I breathe into his face. "Don't."

He stumbles back, unsure. The Icelander bursts out laughing. How good it would feel to knock him down. I wrest the can from the Frenchman and fling it over the cemetery wall. Then, fists balled, I wait.

Their happy, little bubble burst, they lose interest and walk away. I stand there, waiting, feeling as if I'm guarding the graves and bones, as if at this moment, it's my only job. Fortunately, they hop over the low wall and head into town.

I let out a long breath. It's then I realize that the older pilgrim had followed us. I wave an embarrassed hello as he walks over. His skin is a leathery brown and veins on his neck quiver.

"There are pilgrims buried in this ground," he says, voice terse.

Their footsteps, I follow.

"Any fool can walk to Santiago," the man continues, "but a real pilgrim has honor."

Too wound up to speak, I point to a collapsed grave. He nods. Then together, we collect the skulls and bones and place them inside. We dig dirt with our bare hands and cover the grave. Crickets chirp and the sun sets. After we finish, the man says a short prayer in Spanish and we shake hands.

When I return to the refuge, it's dinnertime, and the Brazilians are in charge of cooking tonight. They hand out bowls of macaroni and sausage stew. Loïc's in the middle of a crowded table, holding court as usual, making everyone laugh. Several women might or might not be falling in love. They sure do look smitten. I wave to him and he winks in response.

Felipe, the pilgrim from Madrid, is here. I haven't seen him since our first night in Larrasoña. He runs over and gives me a hug.

"*Amigo,*" he says, practically beaming. "The book."

"Book?" I ask, joining him at his table.

"The *Gita,*" he says.

Oh yeah, I forgot all about that. I nod. "Like it?"

"Like it? My heart, for the first time in years, it is light."

"Really?"

"It is about living what you were created for. And for me, that is physics. I have decided I will sell my company and go to university for my PhD."

"Wow," I say, "you're returning to your atoms."

He smiles. "The Camino brought me what I needed. Through you."

The Camino becomes a part of you, Roseangela had said. What she didn't mention was that you, in turn, became a part of it.

I share this later in the night with Loïc. He places a hand on my shoulder, smiles deeply.

"Magic, *mon ami.* It has started."

## Day Seventeen

Rain lashes against us from all sides. We walk single-file, heads lowered, ponchos brushing against green wheat stalks. The wind howls between lightning strikes. Fields stretch out to the horizon and clouds drift above in layers, darker and darker shades of gray.

Loïc overtakes me just as I sink a foot into mud, trip, and catch myself. He can't help but laugh at the look of pure misery on my face. Water seeps into my boots. Inside, they feel like floating pools where generations of fish live, spawn, and die. Outside, they are covered in mud. It is like walking with weights attached to your feet.

The weather has been the same for days and everything I have, including myself, is soaked. Sometimes the rain never seems to end, and other days, it comes in spurts as we sit in bars, a drink in our hands, waiting out the downpour. I hope today will be one of those days.

Frustrated with our slow progress, I speed up and pass Loïc until he is a blue-poncho speck behind me. The path turns into a road and leads through a village, and, thankfully, a bar. I take my poncho and pack off, leaving them by the door, and sit near the window. A woman comes out of the back room, wipes her hands on her apron, and takes my order. Soon I am watching the rain, a plate of cheese and ham and a cup of hot chocolate in front of me.

Yesterday afternoon, I finally gave in and called Sue. She was on her way out but picked up. "I knew it was you," she said. I told her that I missed her. She didn't respond, and when I started to say more, she stopped me. "You left," she said, her voice tight. "I'm sorry, but I need to go on with my life."

"Do you love what's-his-name?"

A long silence, so rather than draw out the answer I was afraid of, I told her that I had to go, my calling card was running out. "Okay," she said. "But you called me collect. Well, keep in touch." She hung up. Keep in touch? Like what, smoke signals? Christmas cards?

Even if I wanted to, it's impossible to blame her. So I blame what's-his-name instead. I blame him for taking advantage of my lack of commitment. For my losing her. For the rain, the mud, the cold, the aches in my legs, the painful marks on my shoulders rubbed raw from the straps on the backpack. That passes time, but wears itself out. So now I blame myself, which is easy to do on a day like this. A few minutes later, Loïc walks by slowly. I'd rather be alone, but no luck. He notices me through the window, waves, and comes inside.

He stamps his boots at the door, removes his gear, orders

at the counter, and sits down heavily in the green plastic chair across from mine.

"Aaah," he breathes out.

The woman brings his *café con leche* and he drinks it in slow, halting sips. He makes small talk while rain patters against the window. Leaves drift in the narrow gutters, water drips from the awning over the door.

"You seem cross," he finally says. "Maybe the weather does not agree with you."

The stubble on his face is long enough to be the beginnings of a beard. As he waits for me to say something, I realize just how fond I've become of this man.

"I've been thinking."

"I have noticed. A very agreeable hobby."

"When you leave things behind, sometimes they leave you behind also."

"You refer to sentimental things? A woman?"

"It's that obvious?"

He takes a sip, laughs. "I shall be generous and say no."

The wind blows rain in through the doorway. He sets the cup aside, rubs his cheek.

"Life can become complicated. Relationships between men and women are not so easy, too. But to be with a woman, it is a very pleasurable and agreeable part of life. You must follow my advice where this matter is concerned."

I shrug. Tell me something I don't know.

"Well." He folds his arms. The chair creaks. "Maybe this is far too serious a matter to leave it to a seafarer."

I force myself to grin. "No, go on."

He looks pleased. He presses both palms on the table. "I said this to make you smile, because nothing is important enough to put you in a bad situation."

"How's this?" I say and fill him in on Sue, the whole thing.

"Well," he says once I've worn myself out, "you could spend the night playing the guitar under her window. And I can assure you, it will be more than one night. I am sure of it."

"I doubt it'll work," I say. "Thing is, I thought I wanted my freedom. I figured committing would hold me—"

"But freedom has a price," he says, smile gone. "Freedom also means being free to love."

I shrug again. My go-to gesture for the day.

"Well, it's not difficult to find ladies who want to share things, maybe your bed. But to be with the right lady, now that is not easy." He clears his throat, crumples the napkin. "Before the Camino, I went to dinner with a friend and his wife. They are not happy with each other but they never talk about it. They will stay together to the end of their lives, foreigners to each other, quiet but aggressive."

The rain is coming down in sheets.

"I think that before you choose a girl, you must be quite well in your skin. Then the right girl will connect to your true self instead of one who appeals to your nervosa. It took me a long time to discover that."

"Loïc, she's with what's-his-name and I—"

"What is his name?"

"What's-his-name."

He sighs loudly. I can actually feel it.

"Listen. We can either be a Frenchman and American discussing politics or I can be your friend. Which do you prefer?"

Hands up, I make an exaggerated surrendering gesture. "Friends."

"Good," he says. "She chose him. He has a name. When you accept her choice, you are free."

"Not so easy, man."

"Nothing anyone does is *to* you. She is on her Camino. You are on your Camino, and perhaps, they no longer intersect. Do you love her?"

"Yes."

"Then love her."

"I do," I say.

He shakes his head. "If what makes her happy is not you, it is fine. This is love."

"Damn," I say. "That's hard."

"It's not loving that hurts. It's *not* loving that hurts."

Man oh man oh man. I look away so he can't see me blinking the tears. He lets me be.

"I was planning to go to med school, probably far away, and her entire family was in New York and you know I—"

"You are making a list of facts. That is fear. With love, facts become irrelevant."

The gutters flow, the awnings drip, a car splashes through a puddle. Sounds of water everywhere.

"I think I was a coward," I say quietly.

"Very stupid habit, I assure you. The more you close your heart, the more often it is broken. It is humorous, this irony of life."

He leans forward, taps my chest.

"May I be a true friend?"

"Please."

"To think your hurt is special is nonsense. You have pain, I have pain. The world has stories of pain."

I raise my hand to respond, but let it drop.

"*Il n'est pas votre blessure qui vous rend spécial.*"

Then he leans back, waits.

"Yes?"

"It is not your wound that makes you special."

A kind smile grows on his tired face.

"It is the light that shines through that does."

The wind whistles down the narrow street. It rushes in through the doorway, blows napkins off the table.

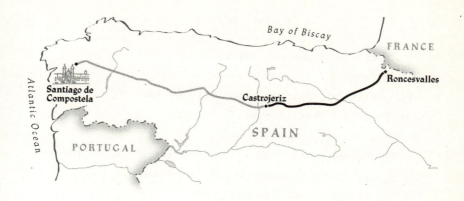

## Day Eighteen

The road descends sharply into a lush valley, past the remains of a monastery, and levels off with rows of thick poplars along the sides. The leaves are wet and when the breeze shakes them, it feels like gentle rain. There is no traffic and birds chirp.

"I like this very much," Loïc says quietly, walking by my side.

Moments like this with an open sky and a great friend, there's no other place I'd rather be.

"So," I say, "I might have a slight crush on a pilgrim."

"Excellent."

"She's out of my league, though. A little older. Definitely wiser."

"A woman will always be wiser than you," he says. "Especially in matters of the heart. *Mon ami*, you will save yourself decades of suffering once you accept this."

"She's Brazilian."

He nods appreciatively. "Good choice."

Up ahead is a village with a church tower, a tall red-and-white crane, and houses clustered together. A white sign on the side of the road gives the name: Castrojeriz.

"And if I'm making a mistake?"

"Fortunately you are young," he says. "If it makes you feel better, you will make more mistakes. Worse ones."

"How's that supposed to help me?"

He bursts out laughing. "That was not my intent. My hope, yes."

I laugh, then remember that word. The first time I called my father after his diagnosis, I asked if there was anything I could do.

"Hope," he said. "You can give me hope."

So forever ago. What had my father meant?

Loïc watches me intently. "Your mood, it has shifted again."

I shake it off.

"So, crushes on women."

"Oh," he says, "the sense of a woman's skin against yours. There is no comparable feeling. Not even good food or drink."

He's playing along and I smile to let him know I appreciate it.

"Not even, like, the best French wine?"

He mulls it over, he really does. Apparently, that's a valid question.

"It depends on the wine. But to be better than a woman"—he kisses his lips with his thumb and forefinger—"it should be like the blood of Christ."

Past the rooftops of Castrojeriz, the land is flat, then rises up like a cliff. To the right, a browned hill with the ruins of a castle. We enter the village and walk through the narrow streets to the refuge.

Inside, there are water stains on the walls, it smells like wet pine, and I can see my breath. A group of pilgrims stand near the entrance and sing in Spanish. A heavyset man with a dark beard down to his stomach faces them and conducts, his arms waving madly.

The scene reminds me of Ron. I miss the Englishman who chased ghosts during the day and sang and cried at night. Each pilgrim, no matter how little time you spend together, leaves an imprint. That, I'm starting to realize, makes this walk different.

When the show finishes, the man collects the song sheets and comes over to the check-in desk. Thick, square glasses cover the top half of his face, while his beard covers the rest. He stamps our *credenciales*, collects the fee, then points Loïc up the stairs.

"Come," Loïc says and starts climbing.

The man places both hands on my shoulders and turns me toward the bunkroom on the left. Through the dark doorway, I see clotheslines hanging across the walls. The room is divided into separate areas, each like a cramped train compartment with four beds. Except here, there are no windows, no rolling hills, no clickity-clack of the tracks. Only gray cement.

Loïc stops. "No," he says to the *hospitalero*. "He is with me."

Hands still on my shoulders, the man grunts and pushes me toward the dark room, almost making me stumble. Loïc drops his pack and bounds down the stairs.

"We are friends," he says, eyes on the *hospitalero*. "We stay together."

The man straightens. He is a head taller than Loïc and twice as wide.

"It's all right," I say to Loïc. "I just want to sleep anyway."

"No. Friends stay together."

We had peeked up the stairs earlier while waiting. It was far nicer, with wooden floors, a lofted ceiling, bunk beds, and lots of windows.

"Listen," I say to Loïc. "It's no big deal."

He walks up the stairs, grabs his pack, and comes down. I follow him into the cement room and we throw our packs on empty bunks.

"Thanks. But you don't need to—"

"The *hospitalero*," he whispers, glancing around, "he likes to control things."

"Maybe he's a fascist," I say.

That seems to cheer him up. "Yes, yes, of course. A refuge run by a fascist. A Camino fascist. It is stupid, of course. Such rules on the Camino. What is the use?"

After dinner, I curl up in my bunk and listen to pilgrims snore, the sound loud and echoing. In the dark compartment, alone again with my thoughts.

When I visited my father, Sue came with me. We stood outside the row of small, brick apartment buildings. Each stacked next to one another like toy boxes. She kissed me softly on the cheek, then went to the nearby grocery store to wait. This, I wanted to do alone.

I took a breath, entered, and walked up the stairs as the steel door shut behind with a loud thwack. The stairs were a metallic gray and the paint was peeling. A dirty footprint on the first stair.

Fourth floor, apartment C. The door was open. Someone was talking inside. I knocked and heard a raspy voice: "Come in."

I looked in—slowly. A wheelchair across from me, folded, blue seat sagging between wheels. A walker to my right: bright, shiny, pale rubber ends. It took everything I had not to turn around and run away.

He sat on a couch against the wall, phone propped against his ear. Another couch perpendicular to his, a coffee table in the middle. He glanced up and smiled.

"You are here," he said. It sounded like a question.

He wore a white T-shirt and white pants, but the way they fell about him, he was like a man wearing curtains. A blue Yankees baseball cap on his head. We shook hands, his curling softly inside mine. Through the door to the bedroom, I saw walls covered with photos, books, the assorted mess of a man's life. A man I only knew as a memory.

His eyes followed my every move. He hung up the phone, offered me food or something to drink.

"I already ate," I told him. "A huge meal." A lie.

"Eat a little," he said. "Have a taste."

I patted my stomach. "I'm stuffed."

I was too afraid. To get close, to eat from his plate, drink from his cup.

There were lapses in the conversation and I almost fell asleep, tired from having stayed awake the night before. There was a tree outside the window. The sky was a light blue and the leaves shook. In a city of concrete, where did the wind come from?

He stood and went to the bedroom using the walker. It was

a slow process: he held it with tense arms, leaned his weight on the metal, and took inching steps. It was endless, but I saw triumph on his face. He rummaged through his closet and offered me a shirt.

"I always buy everything in twos," he said.

I couldn't do it, instead making an excuse about pick-·ing out my own clothes. He replaced the shirt on the hanger and nodded. In that moment, I understood that he knew and something inside me twisted. Still, I couldn't.

"You look like you exercise often, my boy." He patted my shoulder. "I am very impressed by your physique."

His body was thin and frail. Large hands attached to skinny arms. A catheter stuck out of his chest, like a tiny spear. I remembered the night he called me about it. The surgical resident had put it in wrong and had to repeat the painful procedure.

"They are butchering me," he said, voice cracking. "Butchering me."

Standing next to him, I felt hate build for the profession I'd chosen, how the medical system destroyed a body to try and save it.

"Look at that." He gestured to a passport-style photo of him on the bedside table. Hair combed back, shirt and tie, face not so thin. "Taken last year. When I was fine."

He paused, lost in thought.

"Fate is a strange thing."

Finally, for the first time since I walked in, I looked at his eyes. Sunken, tired, and yet, the same ones I remembered. The shouting. The hitting. I was terrified of those eyes. But instead of the old fear, I felt a deep unease, a twinge of anger.

He returned to his couch in the living room. He said that he planned to see the New Year's celebration four years later. In the same breath, he leaned forward and asked me to take his ashes to India, to continue the tradition of his ancestors. Our ancestors.

I laughed an uncomfortable laugh.

"Let's talk about it in four years," I said.

Months later, he passed away. And before I knew it, here I am, somewhere deep in the bowels of Spain, wide awake in a dark room resembling a prison. There is a reason why I'm here, Loïc had said, and it will make sense someday.

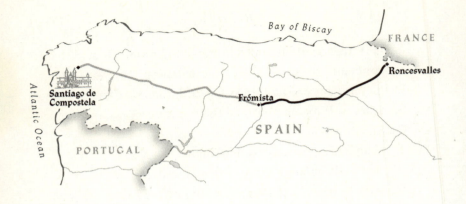

## Day Nineteen

We are on a clay trail winding past rows of tilled earth. There are no crops in the fields. The wind picks up fine pieces of sand and clay. It is like walking through a thin, red mist.

I'm with an Episcopalian minister from North Carolina. He's a quiet and thoughtful guy, not bad qualities for a priest. He tells me about his parish, and how even though he misses them, it is good to be away.

"Can I ask you a question?"

For a moment, I feel foolish. Here he is on vacation and I'm asking him to work. But he smiles, putting me at ease. It's one of the warmest smiles I've ever seen: gentle and slow, it spreads across his face and through his beard until even the fine lines around his eyes stretch.

"Sure."

"Why is there suffering?"

The smile fades slightly and he studies me. The expression on his face is kind.

"You might want to be more specific," he finally says.

"I'm thinking of my father," I say. "I can accept that he had to die. It's a part of life. What I can't understand is his cancer. Why did his body have to be torn apart? No one, no one should suffer that way."

The wind picks up again. I taste the clay grit on my lips and squint.

"This question of suffering," he says, his southern accent rising over the wind, "it's the age-old one. In the book of Job, the writer asks the same question. Have you read *The Brothers Karamazov*?"

I nod.

"Dostoevsky asks: if there is a loving God, then why does suffering exist?" He runs a hand through his beard. "A week before I left for Spain, I attended a funeral for a young man who'd just graduated from high school. He had his whole life ahead of him. He died in a car accident. What do I tell his family? How do I console them?"

Farther ahead, Loïc is laughing with the minister's two pre-teen sons.

"To tell you the truth," the minster says, "I'm not sure if anyone's got the right answer. So maybe, we need to ask a different question."

"What's that?"

"Well, you could try the 'whys'—Why me? Why now? Why here? Why this?—but I don't believe you'll find what you're looking for. Try this: ask, 'Now what? Now that this has happened, what do I do?'"

The wind howls over barren fields.

"People have this amazing resiliency, this power to live through the worst things imaginable—famine, genocide, you name it—and still they survive. Not only survive, but sometimes flourish. How? How do they do it? I would venture that it's not by focusing on the 'why?' but moving ahead with the 'now what?' You might want to try that."

He sips from his bottle.

My father died.

*Now what?*

He suffered alone and I did nothing.

*Now what?*

With the eyes of a child, I looked at my father and saw someone to fear. With the eyes of an adult, I saw him as a man who suffered. With the eyes of a son, I watched him die.

*Now what?*

I don't know the answer, but each time I ask the question, I feel a little lighter. I can't change what happened, but what will I do with it? The answer, I know, depends upon me.

He's waiting for me to say something.

"I felt so helpless after his death," I say. "I wanted to solve things, make up for mistakes—both his and mine—but I couldn't. But maybe I can choose what's going to come out of this."

He smiles a wide smile. "Perhaps you already have."

We reach the refuge in Frómista just as the sun dips below the roofs of the village. The *hospitalero* notices me opening empty closets and asks what I am doing. When I tell him that I'm looking for blankets, he asks what happened to my sleeping bag.

"Don't have one," I say.

"No sleeping sack?" He smacks his forehead. "Are you crazy?"

He calls a man over from the kitchen and says something in fast Spanish, making them look me over and laugh. "Do you realize where you are going?" the *hospitalero* asks, his voice high. "The mountains. Mountains! It will be cold. The refuges have no blankets." He wags a finger. "*You* will be very cold."

I shrug and walk away.

"Wait," he shouts. "You do not care?"

I go down the stairs without replying. The man is talking to an accidental pilgrim who's spent the last few months bouncing around without plans or the right gear. Things work themselves out.

Frómista has several churches, not much of a surprise for anyone on the Camino. It doesn't matter if a village possesses two cows, ten chickens, and three people. It has a church. Some have two or three, while every city seems to have a cathedral.

I find Loïc in one, sitting in a back pew, during the evening mass, and join him. There are a few old men and women following the priest, who stands at the altar, reciting quickly, pausing while the parishioners mumble in unison, then reciting again. It's a world away from the priest who made the garlic soup. When we walk out, Loïc is quiet.

"You're going to miss this, aren't you?" I ask. Yesterday he found out that he had to return to work. Today would be his last day on the Camino.

He smiles, looking tired. The creases under his eyes deepen.

"Come on," I say, "we need to find a bar, have a bottle of wine."

"Yes, yes, of course," he says, then grins. "I am proud of you. Now you are thinking like a Frenchman."

At night, after a couple bottles of wine, I lie in a sleeping bag, courtesy of a pilgrim who decided to stay in a hostel with clean sheets, blankets, and hot water. Loïc snores softly in the adjacent bunk. Tomorrow, while I walk west, he will take the bus to Burgos, then a train to Paris. I will miss him. A lot. I think of the people I have met, the miles we walked together, the experiences we shared, and now they are gone.

Give a person a few squiggly lines or an assortment of dots, and he will find a pattern. A natural attempt to make sense of randomness. When I look back at this journey, I still see just a series of occurrences. In less than a day, the Camino de Santiago will be a memory for Loïc, something to ponder in a free moment. He will have the luxury of one thing I don't possess: perspective.

A car passes outside, headlights arcing through the window. Shadows slide along the wall. Feeling sad and a little lonely, I think of Sue and Roseangela, and when it seems like I just shut my eyes, Loïc is gently shaking me. It's already light outside.

"Sorry to wake you," he says, "but I wanted to say goodbye."

"No, no," I say, blinking the sleep away. "Glad you did." I stand up, groggy. "I will miss you, Loïc."

He nods. "I hope you come to Paris. I shall be very pleased to have you as my guest."

"I will," I say, my voice cracking slightly. "I will."

I notice his backpack on the floor, my things lying on top. He's wearing my pack.

"Loïc."

He shakes his head.

"It would make me happy to know you have a proper backpack."

"Oh man." I hug him tight. "Thank you."

He steps back, hands on my shoulders, and smiles.

"Your season for fakes is over. *Mon ami.*"

"*Mon ami.*"

He walks to the door, turns to me. Something's going on in his head. I wait.

"I have made many mistakes in my life," he finally says. "Everything I shared with you, it is from my experience. This is my bias and you must understand that. It is that when you love someone, you wish for things to be perfect for them. Even the pain. What you wish to avoid for them is unnecessary pain. That is what I mean by perfect."

I start to say something but he waves me off. A long grin.

"I wish for you a perfect Camino."

He walks out the door. I hear his footsteps on the stairs, then see him through the window, my old imitation Lowe Alpine pack bobbing up and down.

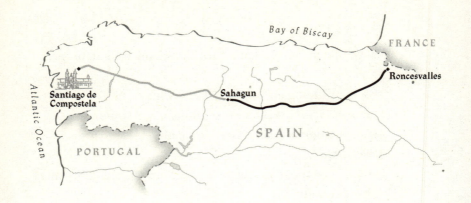

## Day Twenty-one

Two highways, separated by a wide patch of brown grass, stretch past dry, barren fields and into the horizon like parallel lines that grow closer in the distance but never join. They head west. My pack feels heavy and my T-shirt is damp with sweat.

I trudge along the edge of one highway, alone except for the occasional truck. It shimmers in the heat, grows louder and bigger, then passes by with a rush of hot wind. Sometimes I wave. Sometimes the driver blows the horn. The noise ripples and hangs in the air until the truck is once again a speck.

I follow yellow arrows painted on road signs and utility poles. Across the highway is a stone monument shaped like a slim pyramid, with a bench before it. It is white and as tall as me.

This region is the Meseta, a German pilgrim told me. Starts at Burgos, ends at León. The land of Death. Nine hundred meters above sea level, it's the corn-growing region of Spain.

"Here, the land is harsh," he said. "These people have nine months of winter and three months of *hell*." He stopped, said it again. "Hell."

"Let me guess," I said. "We're in those three months?"

He nodded. "Out here, in this land, a man can find himself."

I drink warm, plastic-tasting water from my bottle and rest on the bench for a while. A plaque on the monument states that a special thirty-six-kilometer road has been built for pilgrims by the local county. A dry dirt path, about ten feet wide and lined with small, bare trees, starts at the base of the monument and leads away from the highways.

After my father's funeral, I sat in his apartment surrounded by boxes and garbage bags. It was my second time in this place. The first was a brief visit. This one had a purpose. Everything he collected in his life was here. I had a week to throw it all away.

I came across a sheet of paper with names and phone numbers. On top, in plain ink, was written, "In case of death, call:"

In case of death.

I clutched the list in my hand, and slumped onto his bed. It was a gray, overcast day. A train rattled by. Someone downstairs had the TV on and I heard music. It came through the floors, filled the walls, floated out the windows.

I once had a conversation with him over the phone, me in a warm kitchen ready to go crawl into bed with Sue, him on the other end, his voice strained, mentioning that he was being readmitted to the hospital.

"I am worse when they are done with me," he said. Then, like a child, he asked, "When does it get better?"

I remained silent, never mentioning death, never asking

how he dealt with the pain, the chemotherapy, if he ever craved to be held as he lay alone in the darkness while his body consumed itself. I was afraid of getting close, afraid of feeling. I was afraid of so many things.

A small yellow arrow on the base of the monument points the way. It's then I realize that I haven't given much thought to who paints them. All the nameless volunteers over the centuries, and without them, pilgrims would be lost. I would be lost. This amazes me. Just when you think you're alone, you start to understand that you're not.

My cracked lips hurt and taste salty when I run my tongue over them. Far up, a jet leaves behind a lazy trail of white. There are no clouds in the sky and it hurts to squint at the sun. How long will it take for the plane to cross this stretch? Minutes, probably. I count in days.

I soak the moment in. Dirt, barren fields, heat, wide-open sky. A yellow arrow. I hoist the weight of everything I'm carrying and continue west.

# Day Twenty-three

The thirty-six-kilometer path ends outside the crumbling medieval walls of the town of Mansilla de las Mulas. After checking in to the refuge and claiming a bunk, I relax in a chair in the courtyard. Eyes closed, I lean my head back and feel the evening sun on my face.

Pilgrims walk by, their sandals making slapping sounds on the cement. A woman with an English accent is speaking nearby, her voice gentle and soothing. She laughs several times.

"I tell you what, though," I hear her say. "The Spanish, they remind me a bit of the Africans. I've been so amazed by the Africans. Their beauty, their spirit, it's brilliant."

Then she says something quietly, laughs, and another voice laughs with her. A man's voice, familiar: Nick. I look to my left, and see him sitting at a table with the woman. She must be somewhere in her early sixties. Her silver hair is cut short, almost boyish, and falls haphazardly over her forehead. Her cheeks are red and her eyes are green.

She notices me and smiles, causing the wrinkles around her mouth to tighten. I return the smile, lean back again, and close my eyes.

Someone runs past, boots pounding on the floor. I rub my stiff neck and stretch it slowly, left ear to left shoulder, right ear to right shoulder, chin to chest. Two men sit down behind me, their voices loud, talking rapidly in French. It makes me think of Loïc. You get used to hellos and goodbyes while traveling, but every once in a while, you meet that rare person who makes you wonder how life ever existed without them in yours.

When the men leave, the woman is speaking again.

"…and people had warned us about the customs in Algeria and how you could get killed and such."

I open my eyes. The sky is the sort of darkening blue that comes once the sun has set.

"We had to sleep in the customs office," she continues, "because the officer had gone home for the night. The next day, in his office, while we filled out stacks and stacks of forms, there was this long whip hung up on the wall. The customs chap, he regaled me with stories of how he'd killed men with that whip, and I said, 'Oh, really?'

"'Oh yes,' he said. I didn't know what to do, so I smiled and nodded a lot.

"'You're not going to kill us, are you?' I asked him.

"'Oh no,' he said. 'You're too nice.'"

The woman definitely has my attention.

"I tell you what," she says, "this may sound odd, but I've found it to be true: it's far scarier being harassed by the police in your country than being pointed at with guns in some third world country. They've got a system in our Western countries and they use it against you, whereas in the third world—and I've had guns pointed at me many times—there's always a way out. Cigarettes, money, something. The ones with the guns, they're usually just boys, more scared than you are."

"What were you doing in Africa?" Nick asks, echoing the question I'm thinking.

"Working," she says. "I'm a nurse."

I sit up.

"You're still working there, are you?" he asks.

"Oh gosh no," she says. "Well, I just finished work in Turkey, but I work in London mostly."

"Are you a traveling nurse?" I can't help but ask.

That makes her laugh. "Oh yes," she says, "I suppose I *am* a traveling nurse when I'm on location. I work on film sets, you see."

"Film sets? Like movies?"

She picks up a cigarette from the ashtray, takes a drag. Smoke drifts from her nostrils.

"Yes, of course. I've been doing it for over twenty years. I suppose it's all I know anymore. Gosh, now that's a bit of a worry." She squints through the smoke. "I say, are you American?"

I nod. "Good guess."

Nick's long legs are folded under the table. His sideburns are bushier than when I last saw him.

"You've met Kat here, I suppose?"

"No," I say, then to her, "I'm Amit."

"Of course," she says, smiling. "You have that beautiful Indian complexion."

She stubs the cigarette into the ashtray and starts writing in her journal. I excuse myself for dinner, and when I return to the refuge, it is dark. In the courtyard, the tables and chairs have been stacked in one corner and pilgrims sit in a circle on the cement floor around a large pot. Drying laundry flaps from clotheslines above.

"Come, join us."

That singsong voice. I half walk, half run over and sit between Roseangela and the *hospitalera*, a surprisingly young woman barely out of her teens.

"Hey. Where've you been?"

"Alone," she says, happily. "Giving myself what I need."

We smile at each other.

"My heart, it is light. It is starting to open."

My smile grows.

"Shh," the *hospitalera* says, stirring the pot with a ladle. Blue-and-orange flames dance within.

"What's going on?" I ask Roseangela.

"*Quemada,*" she whispers.

The *hospitalera* shushes us again, the flames drawing shadows on her face. She adds coffee beans, orange peels, sugar, and continues stirring. "We must concentrate."

The sweet smell of the *quemada* mixes with Roseangela's perfume. We're packed in tight, and whenever someone moves, she is pushed into me. Her skin is soft and warm and I feel a beautiful ache in my chest.

"Attention," the *hospitalera* says loudly. She pulls a scroll out of her purse, unrolls it, and holds it up with both hands like a trophy. "This is very important. When I say, 'Now,' howl."

She reads from the scroll, voice rising at the end of each sentence.

"*Ahora,*" she says.

Some of the pilgrims howl meekly.

"No, no," she says. "Like dogs." Then she howls so loudly that I have to cover my ears.

She reads a few more sentences.

"*Ahora.*"

We howl.

"*Ahora!*"

We howl, we yip, we yap.

When she finishes reading, we are still howling. She raises a hand until we are quiet, then fills a cup with the liquid and holds it to her mouth. A man howls. She sips. We howl and cheer.

She passes the cup to me. Just holding it under my nose is enough to make me dizzy. The thing is pure alcohol. I take a small sip. It burns all the way down my throat, making me cough and tear up.

"No," a Spanish man says.

Grabbing the cup from me, he tips his head back and takes a long swallow. He wipes his lips with the palm of his hand and grins.

The cup is refilled whenever it passes the *hospitalera*. After three rounds, the ground starts shifting underneath; after the fourth, I feel like I am floating. A woman in the circle starts singing in Spanish. One hand holds a cigarette and the other plays with her long, dark hair. Her voice reminds me of walking alone through wheat fields, the wind rippling through golden stalks.

One by one, pilgrims leave for bed until it is only the Brazilians, Nick, the *hospitalera*, and myself. The Brazilians take turns dancing while the others sing, clap their hands, tap their feet. I watch Roseangela, one hand on her waist, the other held high, dance in the middle. Her stomach is tanned and smooth. She takes small, shifting steps with bare feet, her toenails painted a dark red.

I want to reach out, hold her, feel my hand on her waist, look in her eyes. Forget everything and just dance, her and I, moving together, feeling and not feeling, the stars whirling above like arcs of light. The *hospitalera* claps her hands.

"Listen," she says loudly. "If you wish to dance, we must go to my friend's bar."

She leads us through town, stopping at an unmarked door next to a pizzeria. She buzzes a bell, and waits until the door clicks.

"Come," she says. The bar is upstairs and empty. The Brazilians don't waste time. One swaps the music in the stereo while the others clear tables and chairs. Then, they dance.

Nick and I stand by the counter, drinking our beers.

"Look at her," he says, pointing with the neck of his bottle.

Impossible not to. Eyes closed, smile on her lips, she's dancing purely for herself. As if on cue, Nick drains his beer and walks straight over. He joins her and they dance, him taking large steps, clomping the floor with his boots, her flowing around him. That smile. I stay at the counter, have a whiskey, and catch my reflection in the mirror behind the bar: a fuzzy image, unshaved, sunburned, dirty white T-shirt, gray hiking slacks. People around the image dance while it remains still.

Then I see it, as if in slow motion, him leaning in, lips on hers. She lets him linger for a moment, then pulls away. He tries again, but this time, no luck. He dances around her, clomping clomping clomping, and I watch until I can't take it anymore.

The music is dull and muffled in the stairwell. There's a loud ringing in my ears when I reach the street. If Loïc was here, he'd tell me to...but I catch myself. He's not and I'm alone. Again. Sue, gone. My chest tightening around a woman who's clearly not ready and probably wouldn't be interested even if she was. I'm still a coward.

I walk past closed shops until I come across a half-finished wall at a construction site. It's as high as my shoulder. I climb it and teeter on the edge. The moon is a blurred sliver in the darkness.

The monk returns, one hand raised in a blessing.

"Say yes."

I give him the finger.

"To all that happens."

Both hands, fingers.

"Say yes."

I jump down, grab a brick, and throw it at him. It clatters loudly on the street. He smiles, but this time an actual grin. He's laughing at me in a childlike sort of way.

"What choice do I have?" I mutter.

His smile softens.

"Sorry," I say.

The smile grows and I feel the warmth again.

"Say yes."

War of attrition with a monk, I'm way outgunned.

I nod. "Okay. Okay."

Then I stumble back to the refuge. I still have a Camino to walk tomorrow.

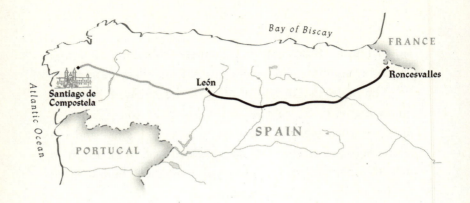

## Day Twenty-five

León is quiet in the morning. The cafés and stores are shuttered and the traffic nonexistent. Kat is outside the gates of the cathedral, a hand cupped over her eyes, peering up at the stained glass window in the façade. Circular, shaped like the rays of a sun, it is the largest I have seen.

I drop my pack next to hers. "Pretty, isn't it?"

She lowers her hand and smiles. "Oh, helloey. How have you been?"

"Okay," I say. "I treated myself last night, slept in a *pensión* and took a bath."

"So did I," she says. "The refuge was rather boring, the nuns who run it take your passport, the real one, not your *credencial*, and they lock you in by eight. I tell you what, I'm a bit too old for all that."

She shakes a cigarette loose from a pack, lights it, and offers me one, but I decline.

"Good boy," she says. "A rather nasty habit, but as you can tell, I'm not exactly quitting."

Pilgrims gather in the plaza, sit on the benches, take photos of the cathedral. One of them mentions that it has over a hundred stained glass windows.

"I say," Kat puts a hand on my shoulder. "Is your neck a bit off?"

She squeezes gently, making me wince, and withdraws her hand.

"Yes." She nods. "Yes, you must be uncomfortable."

"The bath helped," I say. "How can you tell?"

She looks at me with gentle green eyes. "It's apparent to the experienced watcher."

As we prepare to go, Nick crosses the plaza and waves for us to wait.

"Don't bother," he mutters as a greeting. "Bloody nuns *made* me go to mass."

We leave the plaza and walk through León. Kat walks slowly, Nick is in no mood to talk, and he's not exactly my favorite conversation partner anyway. We find an open café, sit inside at a table facing the street, and order toasted bread and *café con leche*.

The TV above the counter is on but there is no sound. Four men sit on barstools and watch the bullfight. Horns lowered, breathing heavy, the bull faces the matador while he sights with the sword and steps in close.

"Ugh," Nick says as the TV replays the kill in slow motion. "Definitely not a country for vegetarians, is it?"

It's difficult to watch but even more difficult not to watch. In the emergency department, new employees would always sneak a look in the trauma room where the bodies lay, waiting for the trip downstairs.

"Humans have a fascination with death," a surgeon explained to me, "we can't help it." Then he paused. "Except when it strikes home."

Kat and Nick lather their toast with butter while I eat it plain, dipping it occasionally into the thick, milky coffee. I pull an apple out of my pack, slice it, and spread it out on the plate.

"You Americans," Nick says. "Always on a diet."

"Just being healthy," I say.

"Healthy?" he says. "I figured by now, after walking God knows how many hundreds of miles, I'd be tanned and fit. But what've I got? Blisters."

Best to keep quiet, like Kat. She eats her bread, munching slowly, eyes on the street. It's a warm June morning and sunlight streams through the window. Outside, a man throws buckets of water on the sidewalk, then sweeps it into the street. He stops once to wipe his forehead with the bottom of his shirt.

We pay the bill and I buy cheese from the man behind the bar. He cuts it from a square block and wraps it in newspaper. Once we are on the street, Nick takes the lead while I stick behind with Kat.

"I heard about the dancing the other night," she says, walking by my side. "Nick said it was brilliant."

Not exactly a favorite memory. "You should have come."

"Gosh, you're young. It's easy for you to stay up late. Besides, I had the runs, which kept me rather occupied."

We both laugh. You get a crash course in stomach issues while traveling.

The city is now awake and we have to sprint through traffic to cross streets. We pass a large building with ambulances idling outside.

"I've got to stop by one of these Spanish surgeries," Kat says. "Get checked out."

"What's wrong?"

An ambulance drives past us, its siren loud and piercing, and turns toward the hospital.

"My intestines," Kat says as the siren fades. "Not a major worry, though."

"Want to go here?" I point at the red cross painted above the doors. "I'll go with you."

"Oh no, dear boy, there's no hurry. I saw a specialist in London."

"Everything okay?"

"Well, I was in his office and he came in and put up this X-ray, looked at it, and said, 'Oh my God, look at that!' and I thought, 'Oh yes, look at that,' and then I remembered it was my intestines we were looking at."

"That doesn't sound good," I say. Working in a hospital you learn that what's fun for the doctor—interesting cases—is no fun for the patient.

"He said it was terrible. He said, 'We'll have to take you in and remove your large intestine, the whole lot.' And I laughed. 'Oh no, you're not,' I said. 'You are a nice man, I rather like you. You're funny. But you are not going anywhere with my intestines.' So I walked out and I've kept them. They act up now and then, but the pain goes away eventually. I can't imagine not having my intestines." She rubs her stomach, smiling. "I'm rather fond of my body, you know. Even though it seems to be falling apart at the seams."

The sidewalk ends at four multilane roads converging into a roundabout. Fiats and Volkswagens and tiny white vans whiz around the circle. There is no crosswalk or traffic light. A yellow arrow on a mailbox points straight ahead.

We see Nick make a run for it. He finds an opening in the traffic, takes it, makes it to the roundabout, where he is almost hit by a man on a moped who swerves at the last second, cuts off a red Fiat, and speeds off.

"Good God," Kat exclaims, hand over her mouth.

He sprints to the other side, his pack bobbing up and down. For a moment, we can't see him through the traffic, and then he is on the sidewalk, bent forward. He looks like he is heaving. Finally, he straightens and waves.

Our crossing isn't any better. Tires screech around me. Blurry images speed by: angry faces through windshields, bumpers, license plates, a smiling baby in a car seat. The world is honks and beeps and smells like exhaust. I don't ever remember running so fast in my life.

"Gosh," Kat says when we are ready to walk again. "That nearly did me in."

"Ha," Nick says, "sure had us sucking on the lollipop of reality."

Traffic zips around. Less than four months ago, I was in the same hurry. Such a different life, so far away. I can't wait to return to the fields where the only sound is the wind.

"This way." Nick points to the right.

The buildings fade, the streets grow less crowded, and soon, we're out of the city and there are rubbish dumps and old factories with smokestacks, broken windows, and rusted metal roofs. Nick speeds up until we can't see him anymore.

I stay with Kat. Her pace is leisurely and unhurried and I have to make a conscious effort to slow down. Funny enough, given how many pilgrims I've met, she's the first one who happens to work in the medical field. The path I wanted and now am running away from. In my experience, nurses are better to talk to than doctors anyway. After a bit, I have to ask.

"I'm sort of stuck," I say. She nods. "I was going to go to med school, but now I'm not so sure. And you're in medicine in such an unexpected way, I thought."

She laughs. "Yes, of course."

"Why medicine?"

She stares ahead, smiles.

"I went into nursing because I thought I wanted to help people." The smile fades. "But I realized." She pauses. "I realized that I did it because all I ever really wanted was to be loved."

That floors me. The honesty, with me, a stranger. Not to mention, you don't hear the "L" word in the profession every day. Then again, no such thing as a normal conversation on the Camino.

Soon, we leave the factories behind. The road narrows and turns into a gravel path, then to a dusty trail. Only the sounds of faraway traffic.

"Did you find it?" I finally ask. "Love, I mean."

"Not where I intended," she says. "I love my patients and they love me in return. But love, it's got to come from within. We must love ourselves first."

Two pilgrims, a man and a woman, pass us, straining in the heat. We exchange quick *holas*.

"And film," I say. "How'd you end up there?"

"I sort of plopped in it, really." She thinks for a moment. "I trained in Africa, I suppose."

"Africa?"

"You'd be amazed what I've got to do at work; I see everything from depression to herpes to major accidents. The crew, they're so tired, so overworked, they don't have time to go to the surgery so they come see me. And I've got to treat them. So I better well know what I'm doing."

"You trained in Africa for this?"

"Right."

Then she's quiet and I don't push her. The sun hangs directly overhead. There is no breeze and I have to constantly wipe the sweat off my face. We reach a town and follow the arrows past a park with a black, spiked fence and to the only modern church I have seen: a blocky, rectangular building several stories high; bronze statues of the Apostles and the Virgin over the doors; a tall white cross in the square.

"Want to check it out?" I ask.

She shakes her head. "I prefer the ancient ones. They always seem like they're falling apart a bit." She laughs. "Like me."

We leave the town through a one-lane road that dips under a highway. It's dark in the tunnel as traffic pounds overhead. On the other side, the land is flat and covered with knee-high grass. Vultures drift above. It hurts to squint up at the sun.

This is siesta country, where people stay indoors in the afternoon and sleep. Heads lowered, we follow yellow arrows to a highway and walk along the guardrail. Three pilgrims on bicycles slow down as they pass us.

I point at the tires. "Must be nice downhill."

"Right," one of them says, veins bulging on his forehead. "But there's always a bloody uphill first."

He shifts gears, the bike makes clicking noises, and the other two follow, growing smaller and smaller until the three dots blend into the blue hills.

We stop and Kat leans on her staff, varnished a dark shade of mahogany, eagle's head carved on top. To our left, past the brush, is a large tree with a thick, gnarled trunk. The shade underneath looks like magic.

"Let's break for lunch."

Our boots kick up dust that sticks to the back of my throat, making me cough. When we arrive at the tree, we unceremoniously dump our packs.

"Gosh," she says, breathing heavily, "this was a jolly good idea."

We sit quietly on our packs, enjoying the simple pleasure of a shady tree on a hot day.

"All right, then." She opens her pack and takes out an avocado, a tomato, a long reddish sausage, a bag of green olives, a loaf of bread, and several napkins that become our tablecloth. All I have is a block of cheese and granola bars. I unwrap the cheese, the edges rubbery against my hands, and add it to the pile. She slices everything but the olives.

"I say," she says, laying the food out neatly in rows, "we've got a proper supper here."

We eat avocado, tomato, and cheese sandwiches. The sausage is chorizo, a Spanish sausage, thick on the outside, fatty and oily on the inside. Pure yum.

"This is great," I say, my mood improving. "Thanks."

She smiles a gentle smile. The wrinkles around the corners of her eyes tighten.

"So," I ask, "how did you train in Africa?"

"It's rather simple, really. My husband was working in Nigeria, you see. When we got there, it had only been five days and his company asked if I could be the doctor of the town. The previous one had had a nervous breakdown." She laughs, then bites into her sandwich and chews thoughtfully. "Me, a doctor? Nurses in my time didn't do that. You just did what the doctor instructed you to do. Well, I said I wouldn't take any money because I was afraid I'd kill someone."

"On-the-job training, huh?"

"Yes, but I was lucky. The doctor, she'd made a list of the top ailments in the area. The two main ones were gonorrhea and malaria, gonorrhea being number one. Before she left, she gave me the list. She said to me, 'If anyone comes to you and says he has a family problem, then it's gonorrhea.' The first time they came, she would give them pills. If they showed up a second time, having caught it again, she gave them a shot.

"So my first day, I sat there in this smart surgery, bottles of pills behind me, medical books on my table, and my French dictionary. I had this smart white coat on and I was so nervous that my knees were knocking against the table. The first patient came in and said that he had a problem with his family, so I just gave him the pills. I didn't know how to examine him, I didn't even know what to look for. I had never seen gonorrhea before."

I laugh. "Not the prettiest sight."

Her eyes narrow slightly.

"I used to work in the emergency department," I say. "I've seen lots of things."

"Ah," she says. She picks up her bottle, takes a sip, leans it against her boot.

"So the list, it worked out?" I ask.

"In the beginning." She nods. "Often, I'd just look at her list and treat the patients. It was simple, peesey weasey. Anyone could have done it, really. But gradually, I learned. I learned by reading medical textbooks, from my patients, and when I couldn't figure something out, I drove them a hundred and fifty miles to the doctor and I learned from him." She pauses. "Well, I didn't plop my clogs off."

"What's that?"

"An expression, from the north of England, I think. They used to wear clogs or something silly like that. It means that I didn't die or do something really stupid." She bites into a green olive. "Oh, these Spanish olives, they're just delicious."

She chews for a while, thoughtful.

"Anyway, what I learned suited me perfectly for the film industry, because there I am doing diagnosis and treatment. They never trained us nurses to do all that."

She finishes the sandwich and wipes crumbs off her lips.

"It's much different today than how it was when I started. That's good, but not always. When we trained, they taught us to do things like changing a patient's clothes or giving them a bath."

I like how she makes "bath" sound like "ba-*aah-th*." So charming, so English.

"Giving a bath was a big deal," she continues. "Especially for the patient. You're so vulnerable in the hospital and here comes someone to clean you, your private bits and all. It was a gentle process where we would do a body part at a time, and it took a while. We were trained to put a patient at ease."

She holds out the bag of olives and I try one. She is right. There is something just right about a salty-tasting olive on a hot day.

"My youngest son, he's a nurse. He wasn't taught such things. They just threw him in with a patient and told him to give the woman a bath. The poor boy, he didn't know what to do. He hurriedly wiped her here and there and that was it. Medicine's improved on some things, while others have gone to pot. I think they've forgotten the most important thing."

I sit up. "That is?"

"Love," she says. "You must love your patients. It's like cooking. When something's made with love, you can taste it."

Love. The Frenchwoman, Loïc, Roseangela, and this woman.

"So every morning, when I'm on set, I fill a steel bucket with medical supplies and I walk around, handing out vitamins to the crew. Something so simple, giving vitamins, it makes them feel cared for. It lets them know who I am. If they know me, they feel comfortable enough to come see me. I tell you what, it works. They come to me. I've got a stool, my bucket, and a wooden box. They sit on the box and they tell me about their hangovers, their breakups, their lives. I hold their hands, I listen, I take care of their injuries. It's a very special thing." She pauses for a long moment. "No matter what one does, there's got to be love in it."

Wherever I end up on this walk, I can't escape it.

"One time," she says, "I was in Turkey on set. My youngest son was there, visiting me. We were talking, laughing. He left to see some Turkish bird—he had a lot of those while he was there—and the producer, he came to me. He'd been watching us. He was rather tipsy from dinner. He said, 'I see such love between you and your son. I've spent my whole life being self-ish. I've never had that.' He started crying. I didn't know what to do, so I just held him and kissed him. The crew walking about must have been thinking, 'Oh, what is Kat up to now?'"

She chuckles, lights a cigarette, takes a drag, and gazes out at the scraggly plain. She brushes gray hair from her eyes.

"What's it like?" I ask. "Being on set, working with movie stars?"

She shrugs. "The actors, when they come and talk to me, they sit on my box like anyone else. But most of the time, it's the others I talk with. The actors have too many people to talk to anyway." She exhales, smoky tendrils floating out her nostrils. "I remember this one, she was a bit of a weed. Rather famous, too. She had with her a personal trainer, her herbalist, her homeopath, and her personal assistant. The personal assistant would cook meals for her. The homeopath, she fell ill and I had to take care of her, which was rather funny if you think about it."

I laugh. She leans against her pack and flicks ash off the cigarette.

"But it's the others on the set—the carpenters, electricians, drivers, loo cleaners—they're the ones I spend my time with. No one pays attention to the loo cleaner, but I think he's rather important. Tell you what, life can get quite difficult without a clean loo."

True that. A clean bathroom is one of the first things you learn to appreciate while backpacking. Especially in India.

"I've got a theory about men and loos," she says.

"Oh yeah?"

"I was on set once, sitting in the mobile loo, and I could

hear the men talking away. Deep philosophical stuff, really. So I've got this theory that men only talk about their feelings when they're peeing."

She waits for me to finish laughing.

"The crew"—she shakes her head—"they work so hard. The men who put up the lights, who build the sets, they work in horrible conditions, sometimes twenty hours a day, and no one cares about them. When I was working on that film in Turkey, these men had to drag enormous lights to the top of a mountain at four in the morning, work all day, and bring them down after everyone had gone to the hotel. Then they did it all over again the next day. It's horrendous." She looks at me with a start. "Gosh, I've been going on and on like I've got verbal diarrhea. I say, I haven't put you to sleep, have I?"

"I'm fine. I'm enjoying this." I mean it.

"Well," she says, smiling, "do stop me if I get carried away. I do that, you know."

She takes a final drag, drops the cigarette, and crushes it with her boot. She glances at the highway.

"I suppose we'd better be off."

I'd completely forgotten about today's walk. I glance at the highway: a shimmering black line stretching into the horizon. We pack the remaining food.

"You know," Kat says, "I recall this one instance when we'd worked so hard, so horribly hard. I worked from half past five in the morning to half past eleven at night. How many hours is that? Sixteen, eighteen?"

"A lot."

"Well, anyway, that night, I took a bath with a glass of wine in my hand, and all of a sudden, I got angry. So angry at the way they work people. Right there, I came up with an impassioned speech to tell the producer. Next day, there he was, sitting off by himself, so I thought I must tell him. Then I thought, 'No, that's crazy.' I went over anyway. So I walked up to him, shaky knees of course, and I said, 'We need to talk.' He said, 'We do?' I said, 'Yes, we do.' So he stood slowly. He was an old man, he must have been in his seventies. We went for a walk in the field. When I had planned the speech, I imagined that I'd sit him down on my stool and say it, but here we were, walking."

Her voice grows soft and I move in closer to hear her.

"I said to him, 'I want to tell you about my day. Yesterday, I worked from half past five in the morning to half past eleven at night. I saw a patient every eight to ten minutes, and the last one I saw was a man in tears from working so hard. A grown man in tears! It's not right.'

"Here he was, an incredibly wealthy man, and I looked at him and said, 'Money isn't everything, you know. You work people so hard that they lose their passion. Why not work them five days instead of six days a week? Treat them well and they'll give you more of themselves.'"

"Did he?" I'm amazed by this woman.

She nods. "For a bit. But the poor man was too set in his ways."

We reach the highway, the asphalt shiny with patches of melting tar. The dirt path alongside is narrow. Kat takes the lead while I follow. She walks slowly, and even though a cold shower in a refuge is the most appealing thing in the world at this moment, I match her pace.

The hills ahead are a haze. Wavy trucks and cars appear,

growing closer, clearer, and when they pass, I see drivers wearing sunglasses. There is no shade, no place to stop and rest. It is early afternoon. We continue on.

When the path widens, we walk abreast again. Her cheekbones are a bright red and the hair above her ears is matted with sweat.

"Can you smell that?" she asks, sniffing the air.

All I smell is heat. I see it, I feel it, I taste it. "No, what?"

"The Camino smell. Like traffic and red wine and cheese and rain and smoky mountains in the distance."

"All that, you smell. Here?"

"Well, I'm making a bit up. But the Camino, it's got a smell. It changes as you go along, but it stays the same, you know what I mean?"

I don't, and shake my head.

"Each place, each country, it's got a distinctive smell. I remember going away and returning home and everything smelled like soot. You'd land in the plane and walk across the runway—it'd be rainy of course, it was England—you could smell the soot in the air. It was the same when you went abroad. Different smells. Karachi: the smell of spices and foreigners. In Dubai, we walked from the plane and I was so excited. I kept telling the children, 'Smell this! Isn't it exotic?' Well, they were probably thinking, 'Oh, Mum's gone off again.'"

I take a deep breath, remembering the crisp air of the Himalayas, temples in India heavy with incense, my aunt's hair, sandalwood. A truck passes and I inhale hot fumes.

"Well," I say, when I can speak without coughing, "right now, the Camino smells like diesel."

"Of course," she says, laughing. "Keep in mind, smells aren't always lovely."

The path narrows and, walking inches away from traffic, we are quiet. I pull a granola bar out of my pocket and offer it to her, but she declines. The chocolate has melted and the inside is sticky. I eat the bar slowly, licking my fingers.

"And you," she asks, lighting a cigarette, "what are you doing after Spain?"

"I'm not sure yet," I say. "I'll see where things go."

She wipes sweat off her face.

"I think you've got it," she says. "If at your age, you can realize that all you have to do is go with the flow, so to speak, you've done quite well. Anyway, I think one ought to have faith that life is going to provide for us."

"I guess," I say. "But I find myself wondering if I should get serious. Start making plans."

"I don't like making plans," she says. "I let life unfold. Well, sometimes one's got to make plans, but I prefer to watch and see how the plans fit in with the lay of the land."

Houses begin to appear. Closed shutters, lawns stained with patches of brown grass. Nothing moves except for traffic or the occasional bird. Then the path widens again, our shadows long on the ground. Sometimes other pilgrims pass us, but no one slows to talk.

The walk becomes one long stretch of houses and multi-storied buildings with shops on the bottom floor, their white walls bright and difficult to look at under the sun. We pass a large house, most of it hidden behind high walls. Security cameras stare down at us by the gate.

"Whoever lives on this property," Kat says sadly, "they must be frightened people."

When we reach the refuge in Villadangos, our destination for the day, our pace is down to a crawl. A narrow hallway inside leads to tiny rooms, each crammed with bunk beds. I see a woman help a man hobble barefoot across the kitchen.

A useful hack from my Infantry days: talcum powder. Lather your feet in it, pour it inside your socks. It reduces friction and soaks up moisture. The result, practically zero blisters.

I tell them about the hack and share my precious supply with him. When I see Nick hobble by, I keep quiet. It's just a little too much fun watching him wince with each step.

After dinner, I join the Brazilians on the lawn. We sit in a circle and they sing in their beautiful, soft Portuguese voices. Leaning back on the cool grass, elbows digging into the dirt, night sky above, empty street ahead, refuge full of pilgrims behind, sounds of singing and dancing and laughter around me, I think of love and of Sue, and even though I no longer have her, she once loved me and I her. At least I had that.

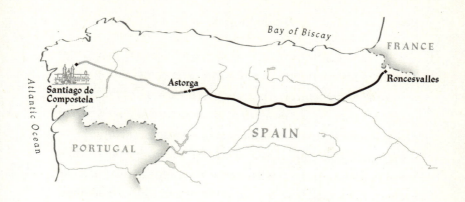

# Day Twenty-six

Kat and I cross a long cobblestone bridge over the river Órbigo. It's named El Paso Honroso, the Pass of Honor, after an incident here in the summer of 1434 when a Leonese knight sent out a challenge to break three hundred lances. All because he was spurned by a woman. Contenders came from all over Europe, and thirty days later, three hundred broken lances. The man actually pulled it off. Then, he went to Santiago de Compostela to offer Saint James thanks for his victory.

He didn't get the girl, though. Maybe she ended up with the medieval what's-his-name instead. Men. I suppose we never learn.

Kat and I walk at a slow pace, but I don't care. It's good to be with her, see what she notices, listen to her laugh. She points out trees, flowers, birds, and names them, each bringing up stories from her life.

With the wind smelling of fields, the big blue bowl of the

sky above, I think to myself: I'm happy. That surprises me. The thought scurries away as quickly as it came, but it leaves behind a comfortable, warm feeling in my chest. It reminds me of when I met my grandmother in India and she hugged me and held me tight, my nose against her warm neck.

We pass a man plowing a furrowed field with a horse, then three women washing clothes in the village fountain. Soon, we are on a small road with fields on the left and hills on the right. The road curves and dips with the land.

"There's so much beauty in this world." Kat stops, turns slowly in a circle. "So *much*. Gosh." She gazes at the hills. "One time I was on location, it was morning and the sun was coming up and the valley lay right before me. There was a misty fog, gray across the valley, and the sun shone through. Pink mist everywhere. I looked at it"—she brings a hand to her lips—"and I thought, 'This is so beautiful. Why do I always rush about so?' The producer, he happened to come up to me at that moment, and I said to him, 'You know, this is worth more than all the money in the world.'"

She smiles at me, winks.

"Well, he probably thought I was a bit daft."

We resume walking. Her stories have a natural rhythm, long bursts punctuated by even longer stretches of silence. At the pace we're keeping, it's perfect.

A yellow arrow painted alongside the road guides us into the hills, where we eat our picnic lunch in a grove of oaks. A large swath has been cut down and only stumps remain. Surrounded by trees, they resemble tombstones. Even the birds, as if out of respect, are quiet. After lunch, we follow the occasional arrows to the crest of a hill from where we can see the city of Astorga.

From this distance, Astorga is an assortment of gray cement buildings, houses with sloping tile roofs, smoke rising from chimneys, and church spires, all enclosed by the high medieval walls. On the far right end are the spires and turrets of a castle, white with gray slate pointed roofs, flags flying. Behind the city walls, it looks like a castle within a castle.

The trail heads downhill, then levels out in a valley, twists through fields, and enters Astorga. Beyond the city, the valley floor extends outward and rises into the hills.

"Well," Kat says, squinting ahead.

"I guess we have to."

She nods. After walking across fields, meadows, and open roads, then entering a city with the noise, traffic, and crowds, it takes a while to adjust.

We rush through Astorga, pass the castle, and even though it's a beautiful city, we don't slow until we are in the fields again. Neither of us says anything, but we let out a sigh.

The path turns into a gravel road surrounded by brush and fields. No traffic. The road climbs higher. Slowly, pines replace the fields and the breeze grows cooler. Clouds drift above, folding into themselves. Kat puts on a blue Irish wool sweater while I zip up my jacket and pull the sleeves over my hands. I never thought it could get this chilly in Spain in the middle of summer.

We lean forward and walk faster. Finally, we see them from behind at the bottom of a hill: the minister from North Carolina with the large olive-green backpack, his two preteen sons walking to his left. Even though I can't make them out from here, I know that drying socks are hanging from the pack and the three are holding hands.

"Oh, those children," Kat says, "they are special. And I do so like their father. He's so unlike what I expected from a religious man. Often, people who're religious tend to be narrow-minded. They miss the truth, the beauty of the message. I know I keep coming back to this, but the message, it's about love." She purses her lips. "Love. It's remarkable how people miss that."

Kat smokes a cigarette, and soon, the three are out of sight. We resume walking. The gravel road changes to asphalt and curves through the hills, the pine forest growing thicker. We reach a stream where the road forks. The main road continues straight and climbs sharply, while a dirt trail heads into the forest. A white sign nailed to a post at the fork reads, "Minas de la Fueraca." It points to the trail.

Having borrowed and read guidebooks from other pilgrims, I know that the Minas de la Fueraca are the ruins of a Roman gold mine. On the Camino, I have walked on roads and bridges built by the Romans, but I've never seen a mine, let alone a gold mine.

"Let's take a slight detour."

She leans on her staff. "What is it?"

I tell her about the mine.

"Oh, really? That sounds brilliant."

We follow the trail through grass surrounded by pines. The grass grows taller, up to our waists, and the trail ends. No signs of caves or a mine. We continue on, but all we find is a large depression in the ground, like a sinkhole. It is covered with brush and rocks.

Kat decides to take a break. I leave my pack with her and continue searching. It takes over half an hour to circle the depression, but no sign of tunnels or openings into the hills. When I reach Kat, she is lying against her backpack.

"Have you had luck?" she asks sleepily.

I shake my head and look around. In the middle of the depression is a large mound of rocks. If I climb it, I can look out over the treetops, maybe see something.

I scramble down the slope and navigate through the thorny brush until I reach the rocks. My hands are scratched and bleeding but it doesn't matter. I feel like I'm on a mission to discover the past. The mound is an easy climb and then I am on top, but when I look out, I only see pine-covered hills.

Everything is quiet. Frustrated, I kick at rocks until a few loosen and roll down. I pick up one about the size of a brick, turn it over and examine it. Smooth, straight edges. When I rub the dirt and moss off, it feels like rough marble. This has to be man-made. I pick up more rocks, brush the dirt off. They're all the same. I must be sitting on top of the mine.

Minutes ago, this mound was just a pile of rocks. Now it's a place where I can imagine laborers and soldiers and horses and encampments, all there to dig for gold. Everything they dreamed and hoped for, a forgotten memory. Only the rubble remains.

"I found it!" I yell.

Kat holds a hand over her eyes.

"Yes?" she shouts back.

"The mine, it's here."

A pause. "What happened to it?"

I stare down at the rocks.

"Time. Time happened to it."

I scrounge around until I find a rock small enough to fit in my palm. I rub it with my fingers and know what I'll do with it. A hawk rides the wind above. I watch it for a while, thinking of bones scattered in the cemetery in the land of death, Romans digging for gold, my father's ashes floating down a river, tearing open gifts on Christmas morning with Sue. Does anything last? I grab another small rock and scramble back to Kat.

"I say." She smiles, looking proud. "You did find your mine."

I hand her the rock. "Here's a piece of what's left."

"Oh, this is marvelous." The smile widens. "That's what's so good about friends. They find things."

We lean against our packs, legs crossed, arms around our knees. The wind cools the sweat on my face.

"Hey, Kat," I say. "If nothing lasts, what is there?"

"Love."

"What about after we're gone?"

"Dear boy, even more so."

I take her answer and fold it deep into my pocket, like a pebble from a gold mine. I trust this woman. What she says, I feel it to be true.

It's time to continue. I stand, hold my hand out, and gently pull her up.

"There's a bar out there with our names written on it."

She dusts off her shorts. "Precisely."

We follow the trail and leave the ruins behind.

"One day," she says, "I will tell you my story of death."

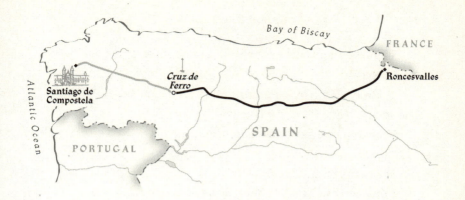

# Day Twenty-eight

Kat and I walk slowly, bodies leaning into the wind, red clay under our boots. The trail, surrounded by bushes and tall grass, curves through the hills. The sun warms my neck, but it's still chilly.

She asks about my childhood.

Nothing special, I tell her, born and bred in New York, parents divorced when I was young, didn't really like my dad; you know, the usual. Then I feel that uncomfortable itch. So I change the subject and talk about pilgrims we've met. The itch fades. Walking to my left, she watches me thoughtfully but doesn't say anything.

"What about yours?" I ask. "How was your childhood?"

Her eyes wrinkle at the horizon for a long time.

"I burst out of a condom," she finally says. "I wasn't even meant to be here."

Silence punctuated by the sound of boots scraping against rocks.

"I always felt like a question mark," she continues, "like I had to apologize for my existence."

High above, a hawk floats in lazy spirals.

"Kat?"

She turns to me. "Yes?"

"You don't still believe that, do you?"

Tiny furrows around her mouth deepen. She moves her head slightly, as if shaking something off. "My mother, when I was six, she told me that she never wanted a child but the rubber burst. I didn't even know what a rubber was, but I never forgot it."

I start to reach out, to touch her hand.

"When I was growing up, she told me one thing over and over: I would never be beautiful and men would only want me for one thing."

My instinct is to say something, comfort her. Whereas I've made a habit of dodging questions, this woman opens herself to me, completely vulnerable. But I'm learning that her stories have a purpose, as if she's trying to share something I need to know. I drop my hand.

"I was a premature baby, you see. Three pounds three ounces and they put me in an incubator. I was fortunate. A loving doctor in Ireland took care of me until I could go home. My parents, they didn't have a crib for their new baby, hadn't prepared themselves for a child. They didn't want me, and now that they had me, they didn't know what to do, so they put me in the chest drawer by the electric fire."

I glance down at her boots: brown leather, black soles, thick, red laces. They must weigh nearly three pounds.

"You remind me of someone," she says.

"Yes?" I say. "Who?"

She stops, leans on her staff. I turn and face her.

"I must have been about fifteen or sixteen," she says. "This was when we were living in Malaysia. I cycled out to the beach; I wasn't supposed to be there. I don't know why, but I went, and there was this beautiful Indian boy."

The way she says it, looking straight at me, it makes me smile.

"He was standing on the beach. I was so shy when I saw him. I remember wearing this garish one-piece swimsuit, it was elasticky and had these bubbles on it. He talked to me. He said that he had to go but to come back in the evening and he would cook me fish."

"Did you?"

She shakes her head. "I went home for supper because I'd get into trouble. I never returned to the beach. My mother would be passed out in the afternoon but she'd be around in the evening. She'd never have let me go. I wonder what would have happened if I had gone?" she says with a dreamy smile. "Oh, anyway."

We resume walking. The path leads to a road. No traffic, just the soft tap tap tap of her staff on the asphalt.

"Where'd you grow up?"

"Surrey," she says, "outside London. We went to live with my mother's parents while my father went off to war in Africa. My grandmother, I loved her so. And my grandfather, he was the vicar. We all lived in the church. A bomb had hit it and part of the roof was gone. My grandmother would go off each day to plant gardens for the war effort. There was a name for it, actually: dig for victory. My mother would feed me in the morning, and then lock me in the attic so no one could hear the child crying. She would then leave and return in the evening."

She's quiet again. Packs creak and shift against shoulders, water sloshes in a half-empty bottle, the wind whistles. I wait, not so patiently.

"My grandmother," she finally resumes. "She found me. One day, she happened to return home early and she heard a strange sound. She thought it was a cat but it was me." She laughs. "Could you imagine, me sounding like a cat?"

I don't say anything. The one comfort I always had was my mother, her touch, her voice. I can't imagine a life without that.

"My grandparents confronted my mother and she told them about an affair she was having with an Australian. She'd been spending the days with him, you see."

"While you were in the attic?"

"Yes, sounding like a cat. My grandfather told her to get out, so we went and lived in a flat in London with the Australian. They put me in the kitchen in a bed over red tiles. I was three. I remember there were rats and they'd crawl over my bed at night. I was so frightened. But I loved going to the underground; they were bomb shelters then. I remember rows and rows of bunks and people would give me sweets and pat my head. I got so much love from the people there."

She lights a cigarette, takes a deep drag, and lets it out slowly. She snaps the lighter shut. Somewhere in the brush, a cricket starts to chirp.

"You know, I do so believe in affecting the person next to me," she says. "By being genuine, by sharing yourself, you give a piece of yourself to them, they think about it, and then they share a piece of themselves with someone else. That's how you change the world, I think. One person at a time. Oh, watch out for the poo."

I sidestep it. Even though we are on a road, there are villages nearby and cattle are everywhere. Several must have passed through here.

"Did you notice?" she asks. "Life's like that. One moment you're plodding along having deep thoughts, and the next, you're almost stepping into poo."

We both have a good laugh. The road curves and there it is: a metal cross on a tall, wooden pole rising out of the crest of a hill.

"Look." I point.

"Oh yes, what is it?"

"Cruz de Ferro," I say.

Roseangela told me about a tradition where pilgrims carried a rock from their homeland and left it at the base of this cross. As we near it, we see that the pile of rocks is the size of a small hill.

"Can you imagine how many pilgrims this must have taken?"

"Gosh," Kat says, "the things we leave behind."

I run over and climb to the top. In my pocket is the stone from the Roman gold mine. I sit on the pile, lean against the wooden pole, then add mine to the rest. An ancient stone on an ancient monument. I like that.

On my way down, I stop halfway and brush my hands over the stones. They're all different: jagged; smooth; color of sand; black like charcoal. The number of pilgrims over the centuries it must have taken to create this, stone by stone, each carried for hundreds of miles. All of us, as Loïc would say, with our wounds, and all of us, working to shine our light.

I'm not the first person on the planet with an abusive father. Nor am I the only one special enough to be confused about what to do with his life. Loïc wasn't the first one to hit bottom. Roseangela wasn't the first to experience heartbreak. Ron wasn't the first to lose a loved one. Kat wasn't the first with an unloving mother. Even in the eleventh century, a pilgrim had joys and pain, just like the ones of today. The details may have differed, but the things that make us human stay the same.

While I stand there, having my little moment, feeling rather proud of myself and wondering what Loïc would think of it, Kat drops her rock at the edge of the hill and continues on. I can't help but laugh. So like her: no pomp or show, just chuck the bloody rock and move on.

I scramble down, dust off my pants, and squint up at the cross. Somewhere in that pile is a rock from Roseangela, one from Ron's previous trip on the Camino, three from the mayor of Larrasoña. People I will most likely never meet again.

I leave to catch up with Kat. Soon, the Cruz de Ferro is hidden behind the hills. We walk together slowly, neither saying anything. After she has smoked two cigarettes, I go for it.

"Your mother," I ask. "You keep in touch?"

"She died."

"Oh, sorry."

"You know, I remember her being nice to me once while ironing. That's the only pleasant memory I have of her." She pauses, her face tightens. "She was a cruel woman. She took advantage of anyone she could, slept with any man she wanted, drank enormously, and always fought with her husband. She had more men than hot dinners."

I burst out laughing. I can't help it. Suddenly, we are both laughing, giggling.

"I'm sorry," I say, "that hot dinners thing—"

"Ah yes, it's a common English expression." She lets out a giggle, then shrugs. "It's a shame, really. My mother only came once to visit my children, and that was for an hour. She had these beautiful grandchildren and she never knew how remarkable they were. Sometimes, my children, they make me want to cry. I see the beautiful things they do. They're so blooming clever. She missed out on them. She missed out on such joy."

She grows quiet, tap tap tap. Then, lights another cigarette.

"What about your father?" I ask.

"Yes?"

"Were things better with him?"

"He returned from the war when I was four. He came home and my mother said, 'This is your father.' There I was, looking up at this strange man, so I blurted out, 'Oh yes, I have many daddies.' That's when he must have tuned me out, I think. He blamed me for speaking the truth."

She takes several puffs, exhales. Past her are hills covered with heather and mustard, the small, yellow flowers shifting slightly in the breeze.

"We went and lived in Austria after the war, my father was stationed there. All I remember is the immense beauty. We lived in a giant castle with marble staircases and servants."

I watch the heather through the smoke: wavy patches of lavender and purple. Then I remember.

"You never answered my question, Kat."

She hesitates, then shakes her head. "There are two parts of me now. One says, 'You weren't meant to be.' The other says, 'Yes you were. There was a reason you were born and didn't die.' But the pain from our childhood, I think one has to look at it and say, 'It has made me who I am.' That's what makes us special."

"I like that," I say. "It's hopeful."

"It's the only way I know," she says. "We all get screwed up, but it's in our trying to unscrew ourselves that we learn. We grow. Sometimes I think I'm like a sponge. People walk all over but the footprints get flattened out."

She gazes upward. Thin trails of dirty white clouds, soft hazy blue.

"I've lived through the cocktail parties, the lavish lifestyle of the British aristocracy—we went with my father when he was transferred to the Far East—I've stayed at the top hotels in the world and I've seen the shallowness of it all. The people, the parties, the drinking, how unhappy they really were. The whole thing about money bringing you happiness; it's a con, really. Would you like to know where I found happiness as a child?"

"Yes, please."

"The cook, he lived in a little hut behind our bungalow. I would sneak away and there, with his family, I would drink mint tea and share their food. I saw people lie, cheat, numb themselves with money and alcohol, but in that simple hut, I knew joy. I knew love."

We pass a sign for a village, our stop for the day.

"Now, dear boy," she says, "I do so worry about holding

you back with my slow pace and me prattling off. I'm taking up your time talking complete rubbish."

"I'm enjoying this, Kat."

Walking by her side, I can feel her smile.

"That's what's so brilliant about my age, you know. You can talk dribble and nonsense and people will say, 'Oh, the poor old thing, she's gone off again.'"

I laugh. "Come on, you know it's not nonsense."

"Have you read *Angela's Ashes*?"

I nod yes.

"When I finished reading it," she says, "I thought, 'What a beautiful story.' And it'd been about people dying, one after the other. And rain. Pretty miserable stuff, really. But because the writer had lived it, he could write with such beauty and humor. He did not write it with pity."

She bends forward and stubs the cigarette out on the asphalt.

"A painful childhood makes you a better adult, you see," she says, straightening. "It makes you much more of a hopeful person because you look around and you realize that all of life isn't so scary. It's beautiful. And you appreciate that beauty much, much more."

I think about what she said, what it means. I'd always considered the childhood memories of my father as something to run away from, to hide deep within the folds of memory. It never occurred to me that it would make me hopeful, and life more beautiful.

The road leads into a village with narrow, winding streets. Children run by, shouting loudly. Dogs bark through shut doors. A bored-looking woman with green curlers in her hair watches us from a second-story window, then resumes painting her nails. Far ahead are hills, then the sharp edges of mountains.

"Gosh," Kat says, looking around, "this is so beautiful. We are so very lucky."

Sue long gone, bank account rapidly dwindling, still no idea on what to do when I finally return home. None of it depresses me. Instead, standing next to this woman, looking out at the mountains I will have to climb without a sleeping bag, I wouldn't give this up for anything.

"Yes," I say to the monk without him needing to appear. "A big yes."

Then to Kat, I grin.

"We are. We are very lucky."

## Day Twenty-nine

As I pass an outdoor café in Ponferrada, her hand reaches out, brushes against mine, then grabs my wrist gently.

"The refuge is closed for lunch," the woman says.

After walking nonstop the whole day, hill after hill after hill, each growing higher, the last few hours without water, everything feels wavy, slow. I look closer, noticing her: forties; boyish, short black hair; smooth brown skin; almond-colored eyes; long, sweeping eyelashes. Her white top and pants flutter in the breeze.

"I am Maria," she says, gesturing me to sit. "I run the refuge."

"Can I?" I ask, pointing to the full glass of water on the table.

She shrugs: Sure. I drain it, gesture to the waiter for another one, and finish that. When I ask him again, she says something to him in Spanish and he brings me a pitcher.

"Better?" she asks when I'm done.

I drop my pack and sit down. "Thanks."

She waves it off. "It's my job to care for pilgrims."

The waiter returns to take away the remnants of her salad, and she looks at me, lips curved in a smile, as if expecting me to attack the plate. I sink into the canvas chair and feel my strength return. She watches me for a few minutes.

"So, Mister silent one. What is your story?"

I blink. "Huh?"

"You have a name, right? Where are you from?"

I tell her.

"I love New York. I went to university in Tennessee."

"You're from the South?"

"Venezuela."

"That's way south."

"I live in Holland now."

By this point on the Camino, everything makes sense in an absurd sort of way.

"And you work in Spain?"

"I'm the *hospitalera* here with my husband. We are volunteering for two weeks."

She pays the bill and stands.

"Come. Let's check you in."

I follow her to the refuge, and although there are pilgrims lined up outside, she grabs my hand and walks me into the office.

"Shouldn't I wait?" I flick a thumb at the line of tired sunburned faces, their backpacks by their boots, staring at me in the not-so-loving way you would if you'd walked all day and then stood in line for a chance for showers and someone casually cut you off.

"No." She leads me to the large metal desk. On it is a ledger and a bowl of fruit. "You, my friend, get special treatment."

She reaches into the bowl and hands me an apple.

"Because you look like you need it."

I'm not sure what she means or what I must look like, but it doesn't matter. I just want to lie down. We do the check-in routine—stamp *credencial*, write name in ledger, pay fee— then she waves for the pilgrims by the door to come in. I turn to go.

"Oh, Amit?"

"Yes?"

"I also provide foot massages, free of charge."

"A massage?" I squeak out.

She leans in her chair, shoots me a grin.

"A foot massage. I will find you later."

Then she waves for a man to step forward.

I go upstairs, grab a bunk, and spread my things over an empty one for Kat. She'd stopped to rest at a café in the previous village while I continued on to secure bunks for us. Then I take a delicious nap.

When I wake up, it's early evening. My mouth tastes like cotton. A quick wash in the bathroom, another two glasses of water, then I head down to find Maria on the front steps. She smiles and pats the space beside her.

The refuge is built on a hill and we stare out over the rooftops of the city.

"Pretty town."

"Yes," she says. "You should visit the castle, it is very special."

I passed it earlier. Built by the Templar knights to protect pilgrims, it still looked like a military fort. Except for the tourists milling around the walls.

I shake my head. "It's a bit too crowded for my taste."

She arches an eyebrow. "You would like it all to yourself?"

After endless fields and open sky, you start to feel a disdain toward crowds. Especially ones filled with tourists who were bused here and will be bused back to their comfy hotel rooms. Funny, how, even as a pilgrim, you develop snottiness.

"It's a nice thought."

She cocks her head, her lips part. A sly smile.

"Why, silent one? You want to lose yourself in history?"

"Not exactly," I say. "More like find myself."

The smile fades. "It is possible."

"Losing or finding?"

"Both," she says, shifting slightly to face the hills. "I lost myself on the Camino. I walked through mud, rain, cities, mountains, rivers. For more than a thousand miles, me and my husband."

"One thousand?" That's double the normal Camino. It's, well, insane.

"We walked from Holland."

"Why not start at Roncesvalles?"

"My church. I wanted to have mass there, walk out the doors and all the way to the cathedral in Santiago. My husband, he thought I was crazy, but he came. He did not want me to be alone. Well, in some ways, we were alone. Each day, I started first and then he followed, but we met to eat and sleep. We were alone and together."

She gazes at the setting sun.

"Sometimes, when I walked in the rain, or in a field, the whole day I did not know who I was. I just was, you understand? Then there were days when I knew myself. *Really* knew myself." She shakes her head. "Such clarity."

"How long did it take?"

"Three and a half months."

"Whoa," I blurt out. I can't imagine that long. Then again, there was a point I couldn't imagine doing this beyond seven days. Life. It shifts your perspective.

"Yes," she says, casually, as if she's had that reaction before. "But when I finished, it was not long enough. I cried when I saw the cathedral. My dream, it wasn't just a dream anymore. When I touched the feet of the statue of Saint James, there were these, how do you say it, imprints? Like someone had pushed her fingers into the stone. Do you realize where they come from?"

I shrug. "No idea."

"Each pilgrim who has touched that statue. How many millions, how many centuries, to make those marks? It made me...I felt humble. So humble."

"Like Cruz de Ferro," I say, thinking of all those rocks.

She slips her feet into her black sandals and stands.

"I just realized something," I say. "When I went to Infantry boot camp, that was almost three and a half months long. And when I came out, I was not the same boy who went in."

She smiles. "See, you do understand."

While she returns to work, I sit on the steps, and watch the sun dip behind the hills until only pink clouds remain. The rest of the sky is a dark blue. A breeze starts to pick up.

Kat and a group of pilgrims show up. Kat found a pharmacy along the way and bought antibiotic ointment for my eye infection, while the rest had stumbled across a pizzeria.

"They are open for dinner," one says. "Care to join us?"

"Come on," another says. "Yummy yummy pizza."

I pass. Regardless of how much you enjoy someone's company, alone time on the Camino to just rest and not walk anywhere is a special thing. I stay there until the first stars appear, then go sit in the upstairs lounge with a bottle of wine and skim through the refuge's collection of books on the Camino.

Kat comes over, wearing her reading glasses. "Time for your medicine."

I shut the book in my lap. "Thanks."

"It's a bit difficult to put it in yourself. I'll do it for you."

An image of my father in the hospital bed flashes through my mind. His face a frozen mask, his body so tiny and childlike under the blanket, his eyes wide and open and rolling around and around.

My eyes sting and I feel tears slide down my cheeks to my neck. Kat reaches forward to put the ointment in my eyes, then stops.

"Are you all right?"

I nod. "I'm sorry. I'm sort of drunk. I was just thinking of my dad."

"Oh yes?"

"He died a few months ago."

She gently rubs the back of my neck. I feel warmth through her hand, like the comfort of a fire on a brutal winter night.

"You poor boy. No need having tears wash the medicine away." Then, as an afterthought, she adds, "Nasty death."

"It's not the death that bothers me so much," I find myself saying, "it's the suffering."

"Of your father?"

"Yes."

"One of these days, I'll tell you my story about death," she says, pulling my lower left eyelid down, layering it with the cream. It stings sharp. She strokes my head gently as I blink, trying to beat away the pain.

"Thank you," I say through shut eyes when she is done.

"Oh good gosh, don't thank me. I wish all my patients were like you."

She leaves for her bunk. I wait until I can open my eyes and see clearly, then return to the wine and books. Except for the snoring, the refuge is silent.

Maria enters the room and places a large water-filled copper bowl at my feet. She smells like eucalyptus. Her smile breaks through wherever I was. I smile back.

She sits across from me on a stool and soaks my feet in the bowl. The water is cold.

"Shouldn't it be warm?" I ask.

"You ask a lot for someone who is getting this free."

"Sorry."

She smiles. "You are too serious. It is better with cold water. Trust me."

She places my feet in her lap, runs her knuckles along the heels. I sink into the couch, feel her thumbs massage the bottom of my left foot. In the past four months, my feet took me across India and now Spain. The most I did for them was change my socks. Maria treats them like the feet of a saint.

"I walked over two thousand kilometers," she says. "Along the way, someone massaged my feet at a refuge. I was so tired, finished. It was what I needed. When I came here, I knew that I would do this."

"And when you go back to Holland?"

"Yes?"

"Any foot massages there?"

She shakes her head, a little sadly. "It is a different culture. You know, when I first moved there, it was difficult. I am
Latina, and full of fire."

Her thumbs press deep, move in small circles. I feel a tickle,
then it passes.

"The people in Holland, they are too calm. Reserved. In
our culture, in Latin culture, we touch everyone; it is natural.
But there, people don't understand. When I first lived there,
women thought that I was making a move on their husbands.
The men thought that also. But my husband's family was
understanding and wonderful."

I sit up. "You changed to fit in?"

She pauses, cupping her palms around the foot. "No, they
had to learn to accept me."

I lean back. "Good."

"I only change for me, like how I changed on the Camino.
Now I have a strong love for others, even strangers. That is why,
today, I am massaging your feet."

"And your husband, he changed too?"

"It is a funny thing you ask. You know, when we were in
Venezuela, he would fly to the States to play golf. Only the best
courses. And now"—she tilts her head toward the door—"he
is cleaning toilets for pilgrims, for people he never met before.
You tell me if he has changed."

I say nothing. The aches, the memories, the pain of places
I've been during this journey, this woman is washing them
away. I close my eyes, listen to the splashing sound of her hands
in the water, feel them gently stroke my feet. I drift for a while.

When I open my eyes, it feels as if I have returned from

somewhere far away. Maria sits on the stool, back straight, eyes closed, hands massaging my feet. The window is open. The breeze ruffles the white top against her brown skin. She opens her eyes slowly.

"I needed this," I say.

She nods and I realize she knows.

I shift forward. "Who massages your feet?"

She laughs. "I give. When I give, I receive much, much more."

We hear footsteps coming up the stairs. They pause, then the person walks down.

"I have to go," Maria says and removes my legs from her lap.

I sigh. I didn't mean to; it just came out. She grabs the bowl, walks to the door, stops. She turns to face me.

"You will sleep well tonight," she says.

I smile. "Yes."

She turns the hallway light off and goes downstairs. I stay on the couch. The breeze feels nice and cool against my damp feet.

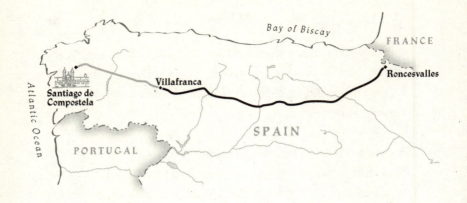

## Day Thirty

The refuge in Villafranca is built out of large, brown, army-style canvas tents at the crest of a small hill and overlooks the town. Inside, there is a bar and a sleeping area with bunk beds. The floor is part dry mud, part flat stones. I find Kat sitting outside on a lawn chair, watching the setting sun. The clouds are soft streaks of red.

I drop my pack under drying laundry and join her.

"Oh, helloey." She sits up. "Where have you been?"

It's been a long day of missed yellow arrows, wandering randomly through fields, and a rather spectacular fall down a hill into bushes.

"I took the scenic route." I wait as she waves at a passing pilgrim, then ask, "Do you have your med bag? I have a thorn stuck in my thumb."

"Gosh, how'd you manage that?"

I glance at my mud-stained pants and boots, then at her. "Long story."

She puts on her glasses, examines my thumb, and takes the thorn out with a needle from her kit. It's a nice feeling to be taken care of, like the foot massage, and I realize, even though we'd agreed to walk by ourselves occasionally to get the full Camino experience, just how much I'd been looking forward to seeing her. She's becoming as much a part of my journey as the yellow arrows. Each seems to ground me, as if letting me know that I am on the right path. She gently wipes my hand with iodine.

I point to a castle near the entrance to town. With the curtained windows, the manicured lawn, and the sloping roof with new-looking gray tiles, it looks more like the home of a nobleman than a fortress.

"Want to check it out?"

"Someone lives there," she says. "A famous composer, I think."

We've developed a running joke about how polite the English are versus Americans. The English being the only people I've met, that if you step on their foot, they'll apologize.

"We'll ring the bell," I say, "invite ourselves for dinner."

She laughs. "Now that would be very American, wouldn't it? You should take a shower, dear boy. This refuge has got the best showers on the Camino."

Quite probably the most enticing thing you can tell a pilgrim. I relax with her for a few minutes, enjoying her story of today's walk, then go to find them.

They are two stalls, side by side, separated from the main

sleeping area. I see a pair of small boots outside one and can hear water flowing. I step inside the other one, remove my clothes, and hang them over the door. A chain dangles from the solar-heated tank above. I pull it. Warm water gushes from the showerhead and disappears into cracks in the stone floor. A woman sings in French in the next stall, her voice like a lullaby, soothing and melodic. I turn my face up into the water and close my eyes. I stand there for a long, long time.

Later, as the clouds shift from red to violet and the air grows cooler, I hike down to Villafranca and find Kat and the others sitting outside a café in the main square. All the restaurants and cafés in the area are crowded.

There are colorful, rectangular designs on the cobblestone square, the borders shifting slightly in the breeze, as if made out of powder. Some have depictions of the cross; others are like abstract paintings. People walk by, careful not to step on them and ruin the images.

"What are those?" I ask Kat.

"I'm not sure," she says. "Beautiful, aren't they?"

They remind me of a wedding I attended in India. The entrance to the hall had been carpeted with marigold and rose petals. You could still smell them in your shoes days later.

We hear music, faint at first, then growing louder. A priest in a white robe enters the square from a narrow street and passes us, holding a golden chalice close to his chest. Other priests follow, one carrying a tall, golden cross. They walk slowly over the colored designs, their black shoes turning red and purple and yellow, while a man runs alongside taking photographs.

Then the nuns pass us, followed by the band—men with

brass horns, cymbals, drums. Behind them, a group of men and women in suits and black dresses, some holding the hands of children, trying to restrain them from walking too fast. The children glance around. The adults stare forward. The photographer goes back and forth, his flash etching shadows on the square.

"Oh, I get it," Kat says. "It's Corpus Christi today."

The procession continues down the square, files into a street as it curves uphill, and soon, they are out of sight. The band fades, then stops. All that is left is a trail of powder, mainly red, dividing the square in half.

A crowd had gathered at the edge of the square to watch. Everyone returns to their chairs in the cafés and it grows noisy again. We go inside and join a group of pilgrims at a long table in the back of the restaurant.

Kat lights a cigarette, takes a long drag, and exhales in one slow breath.

"What a remarkable sight."

"They seemed too somber," I say. "Even with the band and all."

The waiter brings bottles of wine, sets them along the table, and fills our glasses.

Kat holds her glass up.

"To beautiful villages and parades." Then, smiling: "Even if they're a bit too somber."

Glasses touch. Clink.

The waiter brings the *ensaladas mixtas*, then the meat course. The wine is thick and goes down smoothly. By the time I have downed two, Kat is still on her first glass.

Circular lanterns hang from the ceiling, their light

making the walls appear yellow. The restaurant is jammed with customers. Through the large, square windows, darkness punctuated by streetlamps. Underneath one, remnants of the powdered designs.

"Too bad they had to walk over them."

Kat taps her cigarette on the ashtray. "Yes?"

"The designs, I mean. The whole parade, it was like a funeral."

"Oh, it wasn't so bad. They had a band."

"Okay," I say, shrugging. "So it's a festive funeral."

Cigarette smoke curls past her face to the ceiling.

"I rather like them."

"Funerals?"

She tilts her head, laughs. "No, bands."

"I hate them. Funerals."

She studies me gently. "Have you been to many?"

I shake my head. "Just seen too much death. When I worked in the emergency room, when I thought I wanted to be a doctor. Still do, maybe. I don't know."

She reaches over and pats my hand.

"Dear boy."

"Each time," I continue, "each time it happened, I always wondered. The essence of a person—their soul, whatever—when does it leave? I thought that if I watched closely, I'd find out. I never did."

"You feel it, rather than see it. I learned that from my patients, holding their hands." She blinks, then says, "The ones that died."

I smooth the napkin on my lap.

"I wonder what it's like."

"Yes?"

"Death. The actual moment."

She is quiet. I glance up. Her lips are closed in a half-smile. She rests an elbow on the table, the glass in her hand at eye level, and says, "It happened to me once. I died."

My throat tightens. I don't say anything.

"Or nearly died," she says. "I'm not sure. But I came back."

She taps the cigarette, then inhales deeply. Her eyes are far, far away.

"What is it like?" I ask quietly.

"Terrifying," she says. "Completely terrifying."

"What happened?"

"Oh, it was a long time ago. Funny, now that I think of it, seems just like yesterday. My mind sometimes fogs it up. All that pain."

"It's a good way to protect ourselves," I say.

"My memory's just going off with age," she says and chuckles. "But I do so believe that whatever we live through, we do for a reason—"

"Including almost dying?"

"Precisely. One learns things."

"What happened?" I ask again.

She settles in her chair, glances away as she takes a puff, then back to me. It feels like she can see right through me.

"I had a serious pelvic infection," she says. "The pain, it was excruciating. I went to the GP and he said that it was in my head. I remember thinking that if it's in my head, then it's jolly well painful. He gave me some antibiotics and sent me off. As a nurse, I'd been trained that you never questioned the doctor, and I didn't want to make a fuss, so I went home and let it get worse and worse."

She flicks the cigarette over her empty plate.

"In less than two weeks, I was bent over and crawling. Literally. I'd get up in the morning, slowly make my way downstairs, make breakfast for the four children, take care of the guests—we were running a bed-and-breakfast in our house—then climb up the stairs and into bed. I felt like an old lady. It was the oldest I've ever felt."

The soft lines around the corners of her eyes; mouth always laughing or lips pursing together in thought; the short silver hair covering her forehead. She looks out into the darkness, her eyes sharp and green.

"My friend saved me," she says. "Had six children herself. She met my husband and said that if he didn't do something, I'd die. That's when he woke up, I think. I remember a specialist came to see me. How my husband managed that, I don't know. It's a pretty remarkable thing to happen in the National Health Service. He did his exam and said, 'We'll have to open you up and see what's wrong.' They could have slit me in half; I didn't care as long as the pain went away. But I couldn't go to the hospital. There was a laundry workers' strike, you see, and there weren't any clean sheets in the hospital. I lay in bed for ten days counting the minutes until I could go. They were the ten most painful days of my life."

Her voice grows quieter. I push my plate aside and lean forward.

"When they finally did get me in and opened me up, they found everything was a giant mess. They took everything out but one ovary."

A big sip of wine, a drag from the cigarette.

"You died dur—" I catch myself. "You had the experience during surgery?"

"Oh gosh no," she says. "I slept like a top. They put me in a cottage hospital to recover. I remember feeling a bit better and walking about. There were these glass doors by the entrance and I saw a small, round sticker on one of those doors. It said, 'Watch out. There's a Christmas thief about.' And it was Easter! I thought of the poor Christmas thief having to go about and steal up to Easter. It was so blooming funny. I started laughing. I went to my bed, grabbed my stitches, and hooted."

She chuckles at the memory, then stops. Cigarette smoke drifts above her head. The lamps in the square have gone dark.

"The pain," she says, as if speaking to herself, "it returned. It was unbearable. Of course, I'd lived in pain for a while, but this was far worse. I told the nurses and they said, 'Yes, yes, you poor thing. Here, have a tablet.' The tablet did nothing. I lay in bed and sang Christmas carols to keep my mind off the pain. There was this nurse from emergency and she came inside. I remember her eyes—she had really piercing eyes—and I said, 'Please, please don't let me die, oh please don't let me die.'

"She held my hand, looked me in the eye, and said, 'I won't. I won't let you die.' I remember thinking that if I lose consciousness, I'll die. I could actually feel my insides leaking. I held on for almost an hour until the specialist came.

"Then there was chaos. Beds were being moved and I was wheeled into the operating theater in my bed, not in a trolley like that show with the fancy hospital. I thought I could let go, or maybe I'd lost too much blood and I lost consciousness. That's when I saw the light."

I lean closer, elbows digging into the table.

"I was in a tunnel. It was dark and there was a bright light at the end. I was floating toward it. I grew closer and saw a kiosk, the ones where you buy tickets in a movie theater. There was a woman inside, gray hair, sort of plumpish. She was slowly tearing up tickets. I noticed a ticket with my name and she was about to tear it. Then I saw something to my right, almost behind me: my husband and all four children lined up. They had their hair combed and were dressed all smart, like they were posing for a photograph.

"I saw their smiling faces and I knew I couldn't leave them. Who would take care of them? They needed me. It was unfair. My family needed me and I was being taken away. I felt anger like I'd never known before. I would not leave my family! I turned around and saw the woman. She smiled and said, 'It's not your time yet.' My ticket was still there. And then, I remember darkness.

"When I came to, they said they didn't know how I'd survived. The artery in my abdomen must have been seeping, you see, and the laughing opened it up. For all I know, I'm the only person who's actually nearly died of laughing."

She lights another cigarette. The restaurant feels noisy again. The man to my left is shouting across the table, dishes rattle in the kitchen, a child giggles. Who would my father have seen in the tunnel? His sister, whose eyes grew moist whenever she spoke of him? His son, who avoided him most of his life? I find myself hoping that he felt needed while traveling down the tunnel but continued on, knowing that it was his time.

"Can I have one?" I ask, gesturing at the cigarette.

She offers the pack, then hesitates. "Oh, I don't mean to be a bad influence."

"I have them rarely. Special occasions."

"Cigarette moments," she says, smiling.

I take it and light it. At first, the smoke has a bite to it, but I hold it inside, feel it expand in my lungs, and soon it's nice and warm. I cough.

"I won't make it a habit, I promise."

That helps with the worried look on her face.

"How was it like when you were alive again?" I ask.

She grimaces. "I convinced myself that I was better off dead."

"You gotta be kidding."

"No," she says. "It was the anger that saved me, but anger doesn't help with living. When I got well, I was depressed for a long time. But, my family needed me. I fought it every day until I didn't have to fight anymore. It was terribly, terribly hard."

The waiter clears the table and brings dessert. My head feels heavy and we finish our meal in silence.

We leave the restaurant and walk back at a slow pace on the cobblestone road. There is a bright moon out. Kat looks around, at the houses, up at the sky. She catches me watching her.

"You know," she says, "some things are still so clear, even now. I'll never forget the nurse who held my hand; she was about my age. The way she looked at me, I knew she wasn't going to let me die. Also, those tiles on the ceiling. Each time I see polystyrene tiles in a hospital, it nearly sends me into a panic attack."

The road snakes through the town, then up a hill, and we

finally reach the tents. It feels like a long climb. The cold clears my head. We sit in the lawn chairs, bare laundry lines dangling above, the tent refuge behind us silhouetted by the moonlight. She shakes out a cigarette from her pack.

"One more?" I ask.

She smiles. "I say, this qualifies as another cigarette moment."

"Definitely."

She lights hers, then mine, and we smoke in silence. I remember a friend, an intensive care unit doctor, telling me that each time one of his patients died, he would glance around the room, check if he could see something leave. He never saw anything either.

I'm starting to think that it doesn't matter if death leads to a long tunnel with a movie kiosk or if it deposits you into a blank void. What matters is the life we've lived, the people we have loved, those who loved us, the simple everyday moments.

I hold the glowing cigarette in my hand and look out at the dark village.

"Hey, Kat, your story of death—"

"Oh no, dear boy. This wasn't it. That one is too special. One day."

The moon shines over the tiled roofs of Villafranca, the cobblestone streets, the castle. In the distance, mountains rise like shadows into the sky.

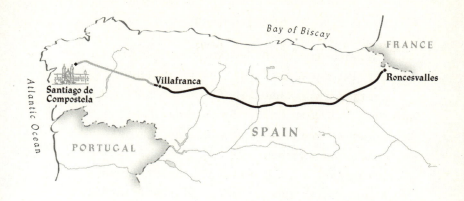

## Day Thirty-one

The horizon is the color of plums. I take a deep breath. The morning air is cool and clean and smells of trees and forests and fields. It smells of things that are alive.

I remove my boots and socks and sit down. The grass, still wet with dew, tickles the soles of my feet. A dense fog covers the valley below. I think back to the Himalayas in India, where once, I had trekked so high that I saw a plane fly below me. The thrill of the moment, already months old, still excites me.

The sun burns through the fog, pilgrims pass, we exchange *buenos días*, then I see Kat heading up the road. Flowered long-sleeved shirt, denim shorts, blue sleeping mat above the backpack shifting slightly with each step, body leaning forward on the staff. I brush the grass off my feet and get ready.

"Dear boy," she says when she reaches me. "You have been waiting?"

"I couldn't sleep," I say. "So when morning came, I took off, but I missed you, Kat."

I put the pack on and feel the familiar weight settle on my shoulders. It's become such a part of my day that I can't imagine walking without it. She smiles and rubs my arm.

"I am so very fortunate," she says.

We walk along a two-lane road. On our left, the land drops sharply and smooths out in a valley, and at the bottom, a river curves through patches of fields. Beyond the valley, wooded hills fold upward into mountains. That is where we're heading.

"Listen," she says. "I had a bit of verbal diarrhea last night and I was wondering—"

"It's all right, I needed to hear it."

"Yes." She nods. "I know."

"That's how this whole thing started. How can I not think about death?"

She looks at me tenderly. "Oh, dear boy."

A small white car passes us, the engine whining as the road climbs. There are rust spots on the rear passenger door. I remember the first time we walked together on that hot road out of León. Seems forever ago.

It's turning out to be a nice day: blue sky, pleasant white clouds, not chilly as long as we keep moving. Soon, a yellow arrow leads to a gravel path and into the woods.

We walk under the shade of oaks and chestnuts, bands of sunlight marking the rocky trail, the ground thick with fallen branches and ferns. Birds call out to each other. The path continues to climb.

"How was India?" she asks. "For you?"

In the forest, a human voice seems out of place. I think

about it for a moment. How do you explain the way an ancient land like India gets under your skin? I think of telling her about the children I saw outside a disco one night in Delhi. They tried to sell me garlands, and when I asked where their parents were, one of them said that his father, a rickshaw driver, was out getting drunk. He didn't say where his mother was. They put garlands around my neck and laughed when I played with them. Meanwhile, young men and women got out of chauffeured cars, avoided the children, sidestepped beggars, and went inside the disco.

How do you describe the noise, the crowds, the colors, cows sifting through garbage on streets, the incredible generosity of strangers, the smell of incense, and the flowers so bright that it almost hurt to look at them?

"I saw this man," I finally say. "He had an amputated leg, right above the knee. He was hobbling on crutches on a busy street, stopping by car windows, begging for money. Something inside just hurt watching the look on his face. And then, the same day, I went to the Taj Mahal. I thought it would be just another monument, I'd go there, take photos, and leave. But, Kat, walking across the marble with my bare feet, feeling that smoothness, now that was something. I had this strong urge: I wanted to live, breathe, eat, make love, and die on that marble. And the symbols and flowers carved inside the tomb, the pigeons flapping against the domed ceiling, I loved it."

I take out a granola bar from my pack and offer it to her. She declines. I chew on it for a moment.

"That's what I remember," I say, "the incredible contrast."

"Hmm," she says. "It is a land of such beauty and tragedy."

She takes a sip from her bottle, swallows. "Do you miss being there, the country?"

"I went there, did what I had to do."

"Oh," she says, "your taking the ashes to the river, what that must have been like, gosh, it's bringing tears to my eyes. It's so special."

I shrug, glance up at the trees. Sunlight filters through the leaves, lights the path.

"What a beautiful thing to do," she continues. "What a sense of closure."

My stomach begins to ache. "The trip to the Ganges, it didn't close anything. I think it ripped something open."

By now, I know her well enough to know that she's studying me. I don't even have to turn my head.

"I realize you weren't close with your father, but it is difficult."

"I don't know why, Kat. I didn't like him when I was a kid. He was too angry, yelled a lot, beat my mom and me. I hated what I remembered, so I cut him off when I grew up."

The ache starts to turn into a burning sensation in the pit of my stomach.

"And then one day, I found out that he had cancer. I told a doctor I worked with about it, and the look he gave me, I knew it wasn't good. Not that any cancer is, but this one was *really* bad. No cure, nothing."

"You poor boy," I hear her say.

I take several breaths; they don't help. My stomach churns. "I went and visited him. The doctors, they'd given him less than six months to live. But he believed that he would survive. First, I thought it was denial, but he really believed it. He hung on for eighteen months. It tore me up inside, watching him deteriorate, talking to him on the phone, listening to him weaken. Not that I kept much contact. I didn't know what to do, so I did nothing."

I stop walking, take another breath. I can hear the thump thump of my heartbeat in my ears. I want to run away, forget about this, but standing next to this woman on a small trail in the forest, there is nowhere to run to anymore.

Her hand rubs the back of my neck for a moment, then stops. I resume walking.

"I came home late one night," I say, staring at the ground. Rocks, pebbles, dry leaves yellow and curling at the edges. Two small footprints. "And the phone rang. A doctor at the hospital, saying that my father wasn't expected to last the night."

I pause and shake my head, a strange sensation. Except for my stomach, the rest of my body feels numb.

"I really thought I was prepared. I mean, I knew the end was coming. I'd heard it in his voice. But...but that night, the message, it hit so hard. All I remember is going into the bedroom, waking up my girlfriend, and crying. I kept saying over and over, 'My father is dying...my father is dying.' We sat on the floor in the living room and she held me. God, I miss her right now. This was a man I didn't know well, I didn't even like him, and here I was, falling apart."

Kat says something, but I can't make it out. I don't look at her. I don't want her to see my face.

"Were you able to reach him before...?" She lets the question linger.

Somewhere to my right, I hear the cry of a bird, then the flutter of wings. I hear the cry again, fainter this time. The sound of wings is gone.

"Yes," I say. "When I got to the hospital, I went to his floor, told the nurses who I was, and the look they gave me, Kat, the look. The same one we'd give in the emergency room to families of patients who were basically done. I know they meant well, but I just wanted to bolt, scream, get out of that place." I try to keep my voice from quavering. "Working in a hospital, you get used to death. You know that, Kat. But no matter how much you've seen it, when death knocks at your door, it gets personal."

My boots kick at fallen branches, and then I realize that I am walking fast. I can hear Kat straining to keep up with me. I slow down, breathe. Thump thump, thump thump.

"What did he say to you?" she asks after what seems like a long time.

"The few times I spoke to him, he would ask me to take his ashes to the Ganges. In his culture, it is the son's duty. I never answered him. I didn't want to deal with it.

"But that day in the hospital, he couldn't say anything. He'd coded the night before. They'd brought him back but didn't think there was any brain function left. He was hooked up to machines left and right. So many doctors, nurses, came out of that room. They all said the same thing: they couldn't understand how he was still alive. He'd been down for a while before they resuscitated him. They wanted me to sign a 'do not resuscitate' order for when he crashed again. I was too much of a mess. He'd wanted to live so badly, how could I do that? I did nothing, Kat. Nothi—"

"You were there," she says, voice soft. "That is everything."

"I don't know."

"I tell you what, I've worked with plenty of dying patients, held their hands, talked with them. It doesn't matter what condition they are in, they can hear you." Her voice rises. "You must believe me."

I clear my throat. "I sat by him, Kat. I said things. How I was terrified of him as a child, how I didn't understand him, even hated him. Then I told him how impressed I was by his fight against the cancer—I really was—I respected that, and in a way, was proud of him. I said that he was my father, and I loved him for that.

"And I said that I couldn't make the 'do not resuscitate' decision for him. His body, there was nothing left. I just wanted him to be at peace. I said that I would respect whatever decision he made, all I asked was that he chose what gave him peace. Then I told him, promised him, that when the time came, I would take his ashes to the Ganges. I would do that for him."

"Oh, dear boy," she says, "he did hear you."

I shrug: Maybe. Whereas once I couldn't run away from the memories fast enough, they've turned into an avalanche. I couldn't shut myself up now if I tried.

"I was there all day. The only time I left was to go down to the cafeteria. I was sitting there, eating soup and watching people eat, laugh, walk around as if nothing was happening. Didn't they realize that a man was dying upstairs?

"Then I looked around, searched for blank faces, empty faces, they'd be the ones who had someone on the floors above. I wanted to find somebody in that cafeteria who'd understand what I was going through, who was going through the same thing, and maybe sit and have soup with them. Know what I mean? Not talk or anything, just sit and have soup together."

She reaches out, places a hand on my shoulder.

"I went back upstairs," I continue. "I sat by him until night. I was so tired. The nurse finally told me to get some rest, there was nothing I could do anyway. I went to a friend's house nearby, and around five a.m. he woke me up and said there was a phone call for me. I knew. It was dark in the living room and I was woozy, and I sat on the couch, and the man on the phone, the doctor, he said that my father's heart had stopped and they tried but couldn't resuscitate him. He said he was sorry but it was probably for the best, given my father's condition."

I grow quiet, feeling drained. Kat looks at me so gently that I could cry.

"He did hear you," she says. "You told him what he needed to hear. So often, people need that before they die. You gave him that."

"I don't know, Kat. I feel all this guilt."

"Guilt?" Her hand squeezes my shoulder tight. *"Why?"*

"Not being there for him. Letting him die, barely ever visiting, keeping the money he sent me in college but not talking to him, not letting myself get close. Pick one."

She leans toward me. "Dear boy, don't you see? You gave him the final gift of being able to let go. That is so important. You are human, you did what you could. That is all we can ask ourselves. You are so very lucky."

That surprises me. "Lucky?"

"Yes, taking his ashes to that holy, sacred place. That was so special. You gave him what he needed."

"I don't feel lucky, Kat."

For the first time, her voice is sharp. "You must listen to me."

I turn and her green eyes hold me still.

"When my mother was dying," she says slowly, "I went to the hospital and was with her. I've held the hands of dying patients often, but I couldn't bring myself to touch this woman. I was a little girl again. She still frightened me. I tried to think of something, anything, that would make me feel love for this woman. A tender moment. There was one: she was nice to me once while ironing. But it wasn't enough. I felt nothing. When she died, my father and I were in the room and I cried and cried. Do you know why I cried?"

I shake my head.

"I felt no guilt," she says, "no love, no remorse. I cried because I had nothing to cry for." She pauses, her eyes moist. "I felt that I should grieve, have feelings, but I felt nothing and it made me so sad. What you did for your father was beautiful. It's something I could never do for her, no matter how hard I tried."

She takes a cigarette out from a pack in her shirt pocket and holds it in her fingers, unlit.

"Sometimes the reasons we do things don't matter. What matters is that we do them. You may not understand why you helped set your father free. Maybe it was fear. Or guilt. Or love. Maybe all of them, but it doesn't matter. Don't you see?"

I think it over for a long moment. "When I was in the hospital that day," I say finally, "when there weren't any nurses or doctors around, I wanted to reach over, touch him, hold him, but I was frozen stiff. I wasn't a man who'd been in the Army and done all these things. I was a kid. But I managed to stroke his hand, touch his forehead slightly, and you know what?"

"Yes?"

"I think it was in his suffering that I realized he was

human." I grow quiet. "I just wish...I'm just sad that's what it took."

We stop walking. She leans her staff against her leg, reaches out, and holds my face with both hands. Palms against cheeks. When she does that, I realize that my cheeks are wet. I blink, feel a tear slide down my chin.

"I do so believe in destiny," she says. "We meet people for a reason, and both of us, we get something from it. It's never one-way, you know."

She lights the cigarette and shoves the lighter into her pocket. I wipe tears off my chin with the back of my hand.

"I sometimes wonder," she says, looking to where the trail bends, "what the world would be like if I hadn't done certain things. If you hadn't decided to walk the Camino or hadn't come." She leans on her staff. "All of our experiences, even the painful ones, are necessary. They lead us somewhere."

We resume walking and she lets me be quiet. The path leads deeper into the forest, and soon, there is a stream to our right. We hike along the edge. Trees with thin trunks lean over the water. The bark on the trunks is peeling and leaves float on the surface.

I pick up stones, throw them at the water. Sometimes they skip, sometimes they don't. An arrow on a tree points to a wooden bridge. We stop in the middle of the bridge and remove our packs.

Water rushes below, and there's the thump thump in my ears again. I lean forward on the railing, close my eyes, try to slow my breathing. My eyes sting. The old childhood fear claws in my gut, paws at my throat.

"Are you all right?"

I know she's watching me. My face is warm, like under sunlight.

"Kat, there's something I haven't told anyone."

I feel her shift closer.

"Dear boy."

"My eyes," I say.

"Yes, I know they bother you a lot."

"My father had red eyes, Kat. That's what I remember. When I was a kid and he'd get drunk and angry, his eyes would get red, and that night in the hospital, his eyes were the only thing in his body that were moving. They were open, circling around and around. The doctor said it was a primitive brain-reaction thing. But his eyes..."

A long silence. I focus on the sound of water until the stream is in my head, rising and falling, snaking, twisting through the forest, growing faster and faster until it is a roar. I am in the stream and it is in me. Then I start to wonder if she heard me. I open my eyes. Foamy water swirls over the rocks below.

"What you're afraid of isn't true," she says quietly. I have to strain to hear her over the roar in my head. "It's normal. You went through a serious trauma and your mind is taking advantage of it."

The roar slowly subsides. The stream is just the stream again.

"I know," I say. "I know that. But it's one thing to know and another to believe. My mind...I can't stop."

"You poor old sausage. You think that because your eyes are now red, you are becoming like your father?"

I watch the stream until my eyes grow blurry. All my life, I'd told myself that I would never be like my father, that the violence would end with me, that I would make something of my life. My father had died alone and broke, no one to love him except a son who could barely bring himself to touch him in the hospital. And here I am, having lost a woman who loved me, no idea what I am doing, and each time I glimpse myself in the mirror, my eyes reminding me of him.

"Something like that," I say.

"But you're not." Her voice grows louder.

"It's difficult, Kat. I can't stop. I don't know how to stop."

"Now look here," she says. "You've got to believe me. The mind is a wolly, but you have to believe that what it's telling you is simply not true."

"Do you remember Maria?"

"Yes, she was very beautiful."

Maria showed me her Camino journal in the office, let me skim through it. There was one section that grabbed me. "All my fears," Maria wrote, "everything I had refused to face now lashed at me. But I fought those demons with a strength I never had before. Some I left behind in the rain, others at the bottom of a hill. A few returned to pester me but I left them in the mud, the stones, and the mountains. I was free."

I tell Kat about it. She drops the cigarette and crushes it with her boot. Then she leans on the railing.

"Demons," she says, gazing at the water, "that is a good way to describe our fears. It helps us realize that what they say is not true. But whatever you call them, you can beat them. I am living proof."

Now it's my turn to examine her. "What do you mean?"

"After I recovered from the operation where I nearly died, I fell into a deep depression. I did not want to live. I sat at home, day after day, waiting to die. No one knew what to do, how to help, but there was this tiny voice inside that told me I needed to live. My family needed me.

"So I clung to that voice. I clung with desperation because I knew that if I let go, I would drown. For eighteen months, my fears attacked me. They attacked where I was vulnerable, you see. Fears are terribly good at that. They told me that I wasn't worthy, I didn't deserve to live, my mother was correct, no one loved me, I was better off dead. Yet, even though they were loud, I forced myself to realize that what they said was not rational.

"Each day, even if it was for thirty seconds, I would fix a rational thought in my mind and cling to it. It didn't matter what it was—the color of the wall in my bedroom or even my name—as long as I knew that it was true. I hung on, forced myself, made myself believe that rational thought. I would hang on until the fears grew strong again. But for those thirty seconds, I had won. I did this daily and the rational thoughts stayed longer. One morning, a year and a half later, the fears were gone. They had lost their power."

She lights a cigarette, her hands trembling slightly.

"I say." She inhales. "I do need this."

"Kat?"

She shakes her head. "I'm not telling you that it's easy. I'm not even telling you that I have the answer. All I know is that I fell to the depths and returned." She stares at the cigarette in her hand for a long time, then folds both arms on the railing. "Listen, you cannot run away. Avoiding your fears or pretending they don't exist does no good. You have to acknowledge them. Remind yourself that they are not true. Hang on to your rational thoughts, which you know are true, and use them as an anchor." Her voice fades. "And you can beat them. When you face your fears, you take away the power they have over you."

She straightens, faces me.

"You did everything you could," she says, "even more. That's why your father couldn't die, not until your promise. That's why his eyes were moving so, they were searching. Just like you felt like a bad son, he must have felt like a bad father. You felt guilt, he felt guilt. Guilt works both ways, you know."

When she grows quiet, I say, "Kat?"

"Sorry, dear boy, I've been prattling along. Yes?"

"Can I have a cigarette?"

She hands me the pack and lighter. We rest against the railing, the sound of the water below, and smoke in silence.

"Anyway," she says, "the trick is not to get so that we focus too much on ourselves. That's when it gets bad. That's when all the guilt starts up. I think that one ought to give up on guilt, it doesn't do any good."

"It's still not easy, is it?"

"Yes, but you must realize that there is a reason why things happen. I've gone through moments so difficult that I really didn't believe I would make it. They seemed so terribly, terribly hard, but somehow I did. We all do."

Her cigarette is finished, so I hand her the pack. She takes another one out, taps it against the back of her wrist.

"Of course"—she smiles wistfully at the cigarette—"I've been completely useless giving these up."

I light it for her and watch as she takes a puff with pleasure. Her whole body seems to relax.

"Honestly," she says, "it's only when we look back that we realize there is a pattern to life and things do make sense. We just have to get through. The bad times never last. Regardless of the pain, my life molded me, and it brought me to this point. It made me who I am."

"I guess," I say. "I'm just not convinced that pain is worth it."

"But you have a sensitivity many people lack," she says. "Regardless of whether you become a doctor or not, this sensitivity can help people. I wonder if you would be like this if you never experienced pain."

"Maybe," I start to say, then stop. The woman I'm talking with lived a childhood of pain, and she made something beautiful out of it: a wonderful, adventurous childhood for her children. She and her husband created an environment where her children were loved and nurtured. One day, she mentioned to me that she'd been afraid her children would become adults without realizing that life can be difficult. But they turned out to be remarkable, and whenever she spoke of them, every line on her face softened.

She lived what the minister had advised: instead of focusing on the "why?" she worked on the "now what?"

"You set your father free," she says. "Now you must set yourself free."

I nod. "I'd like that, Kat."

"You must remember that you did the best you could, that is all anyone can ask. You were able to give him what he needed. He needed to hear that you loved him. He needed to hear that it was okay to let go and be at peace. That is why he hung on." Her cigarette is half ash. She brushes it against the railing, and the ash swirls down to the water. "If you don't believe me, remember that he died shortly after you left. After you told him that you would take his ashes to the Ganges, he could let go. And he did."

I sit on my pack, wrap my arms around my knees, close my eyes, listen to the water. The thump thump has faded and there's only the sweet, rich scent of the forest.

"He is at peace," she says. "You must accept that. He is gone and you are not him, and from what I see in you, you never will be. You are a free spirit. Remember that."

I stay that way for a long time. I hear her flick the lighter twice. She coughs, then footsteps on the wooden planks as she walks to the far end of the bridge. A free spirit. Free to make my own choices, make my own mistakes, to follow my own path. Free to leave the anger and the guilt and the fears behind. Free to ask myself, "Now what?" I finally open my eyes.

"You are at peace," I whisper, gazing at patches of blue through the leaves. "And I'm glad."

The leaves rustle and a breeze cools my face.

"You know what?" I call out to Kat. "I've noticed something on the Camino. When I'm in the middle of nature, and I have a thought that feels right, the wind picks up. At first I figured it was a coincidence, but now I just accept it."

She laughs and walks over.

"Special boy, you know more than you realize."

She extends her arm and I grab it, letting her pull me up. We hoist our packs.

"Ready?" I say.

"Right-o."

We cross the bridge and walk alongside the stream.

"You know, your feeling about the wind?" she asks.

"Yeah?"

She looks up at the trees. "Well, then, listen to the wind."

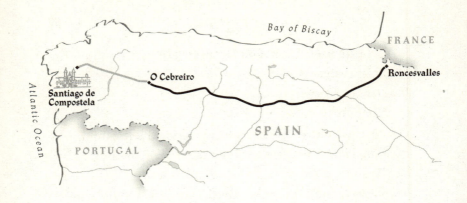

# Day Thirty-two

Through hills covered with heather, a path several feet wide leads to Galicia, the final region of the Camino. A kilometer past the border, a stone marker indicates the distance to Santiago de Compostela: 150 kilometers. The home stretch. Many pilgrims, upon reaching this marker, have been known to sit down and reflect in silence. Another kilometer ahead is the ancient mountaintop village of O Cebreiro. It is one of the most famous points on the pilgrimage, not only for being the highest village on the Camino, but for a miracle that was supposed to have occurred here.

In the fourteenth century, a peasant farmer walked through a harsh snowstorm to receive communion at the church in O Cebreiro. The monk was surprised to see him. No one else had showed up. He scoffed at the cold and exhausted peasant for risking his life, but while he berated the peasant, the bread and wine turned into flesh and blood.

This became known as the "miracle of O Cebreiro." The sacraments were placed in a golden chalice, which can still be found in the church.

Kat and I sit outside a bar, sharing a bottle of wine. It's early evening. In front of us, a paved road heads past the village, and then the land falls sharply for thousands of feet. It is covered with patches of brown and green farmland, and farther, surrounding everything, are mountains rising into clouds.

"Want to see the church?" I ask her.

"I already did," she says. "While you were checking in. I lit a candle for a friend."

I like the thought. "I think I'll go light a candle for my father."

She smiles, rubs my shoulder. "You go do that."

The small church is at one end of the village, and made out of rough stone blocks, like many of the houses here. It is dim inside and my eyes adjust slowly. There is a table with unlit candles and a donation box near the entrance. Straight ahead, a statue of Jesus on the cross on the wall with four narrow windows, then pews and the altar. Lit candles in red glasses line the walls.

A raised tomb lies on one end of the church. On the other, built into a wall of uneven stone, a glass case lit with reddish light. Inside is the famous chalice. I walk to it, rubbing my hands for warmth.

In cathedrals covered with gold and frescoes and priceless art, I found no peace. They were no match for wheatfields swaying under open, blue skies. But in this simple church on top of a mountain, I look at the symbol of a miracle, and my mind falls quiet. It doesn't matter whether I believe the story or not. What matters is the man who, seven hundred years ago, risked his life because of what he believed. Now each year, tens of thousands of people flock to this same church to mark that event.

I hear the thump thump again, but it's gentle and comforting, and then I realize where I am. One day, a pilgrim told me about the concept of a "thin place." They were special places, he'd said, where the boundary between heaven and earth was a thin one. Where one could feel the presence of the other side.

It's the same feeling as when I'd met the monk, the Himalayas behind him. As if everything was in its right place, unfolding as it should. If there is a heaven, then the boundary between it and here must be a slim one.

I go to the table, pick up a candle, and put money in the donation box. As I search around for matches, the door opens and a gruff-looking man steps inside. He notices me, says something in Spanish, and turns to go.

"Wait." I point to the unlit candle in my hand.

He pulls a lighter out of his pocket, lights the candle, and walks out. The door clicks softly behind him.

The draft whips the tiny flame around. Then I know what to do. I walk to the tomb, the candle warming my cupped hands, and set the candle down. Flame flickers, a voice rises:

My father on the phone, his voice thin and cracked from chemotherapy. "I want you to know that I meant well. I always meant well."

Then I am sitting on a chair, him on one knee, teaching me how to tie my shoelaces, me getting it wrong again and again, him explaining patiently, showing how the laces go around each other, then loop and tighten. I remember finally getting it right, and the look on his face, so proud, his eyes smiling, and me feeling like there was nothing that I couldn't do.

The flame grows brighter and I feel fondness for this man who fought his cancer with every breath and wanted to live. He was not a saint or monster. Just human. With all his faults, dreams, hopes, and desires. A human being.

I know some things. I know that life isn't black and white. In between lie hues of gray and entire rainbows. I don't know why my father turned out the way he was, why he got cancer, why he suffered; I'll never know what went through his mind as he lay in bed night after night while his body self-destructed. I don't know many things.

This I know: standing in the church, watching the candle, something inside me shifts. Something small. So small that I barely feel it, but it changes everything.

I walk to the doors, open them, and turn for one final look. The candle burns steadily, at peace, like him. Evening light strikes the chalice, making the gold glow. I walk out into the brightness.

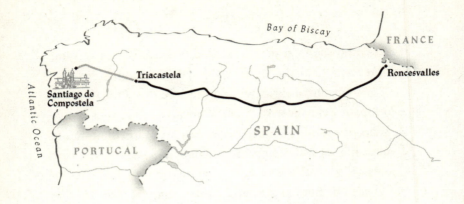

# Day Thirty-three

"Hey, Kat."

"Yes, dear boy?"

"Have you learned anything on the Camino?"

She nods. "I've learned about snoring. The number of snorers in the refuges is staggering. I never imagined so many people could make such a dreadful noise."

Once I'm done laughing, I notice Roseangela. I excuse myself from the table and run over. She's in the plaza, filling her bottle from a fountain.

"My serious pilgrim," she shouts when she sees me, and hugs me happily.

I run a hand through her hair. Soft and silky through my fingers. I don't know what possesses me to do it, but she doesn't stop me, either.

"Your hair," I say. "It brings out your eyes."

Hug finished, we stand much closer than decent pilgrims should.

"How's your heart?" I ask.

"Open. Wide open and alive."

"I can tell."

"And you, my serious pilgrim," she says, "are not so serious anymore."

I grin. "Mine's opening."

She tilts her head. A wildness builds inside. It feels damn good.

"Walk with me to Santiago," she says, suddenly. "We started together, closed. Let us finish open. Together."

Man oh man oh man. If she'd asked half a Camino ago.

I shake my head. "Not that simple."

I tell her about Kat and invite her to join us. She smiles that slow, delicious smile.

"My heart," she says, "it needs to walk alone. But you, you can join."

Mine feels a pang, but no regret, not even for a second. I know what I need.

"How about in Santiago?" I say.

Her smile grows. "I will stay there a week. Come find me."

"Done," I say, matching her smile.

She reaches out, runs a finger from the top of my nose to the bottom. Slowly.

"I'll find you," I say.

As she walks away, I think of the Italian backpacker in Dharamsala who'd first told me about the Camino, how everyone found themselves. Perhaps you found others as well. And they found you.

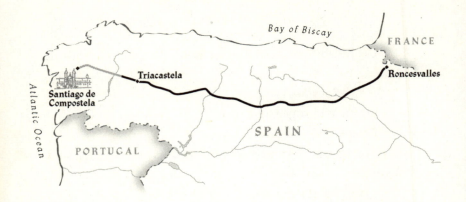

# Day Thirty-four

In the land of Rebirth, the Meseta disappears into mountains and then the mountains slope down to hills and lush valleys. Narrow dirt trails lead through meadows covered with wild-flowers. They wind past fields of maize, climb up the hill-sides, and enter forests of oaks and beeches and eucalyptus and pines. In the villages, the bars play bagpipe music. The number of pilgrims increases and the refuges grow crowded. No one complains of blisters anymore. Somewhere out there, toward the setting sun, growing closer each day, is Santiago de Compostela.

And one afternoon, while walking in a field in the land of Rebirth, Kat tells me her story of death.

"I fell in love once," she says. "It was a total love, complete in every way. It gave me more joy and pain than I ever knew."

She squints at the horizon.

"He was a beautiful man, and I lost him. He died. But in

that time we shared, I learned about the immensity of love, how it can pierce your heart. It taught me the mystery of eternity."

It's a windy day and the field is restless. The chill in the air is pleasant and I run my hands over the stalks as we walk.

"I was eighteen when I got married," she says. "In those days, if you weren't getting married, you were an outcast, and of course, I didn't want to be an outcast. I've been so very lucky. My husband is such a good, loving man. I do love him, always have." A long pause. She coughs. "But loving someone else also, it just happened."

Beams of sunlight shine through breaks in gray clouds above.

"You know," she says, watching the sky, "not a day goes by when I don't look at a thing of beauty and think of him. It's usually the little things I think of, the silly things. Sometimes they're painful, but mostly, just wonderful. I'm a very, very fortunate woman."

A plane flies low and fast under the clouds. Each time it passes through a beam, it sparkles.

"Julian." Her voice cracks slightly. "Julian," she says again. "Oh, he had such a soft, gentle, intelligent voice. It was so comforting." She reaches over, brushes my hand. "You know, it's rather funny, I just thought of this. The first time I was with him, I couldn't speak." She giggles. "Here I am, always taking up your time talking complete rubbish, can you imagine me not being able to speak?"

I tap her arm playfully. "Come on, Kat. You know that's not true."

"Oh," she says, smiling, "you're so good. Anyway, the first time we were alone together, I couldn't speak. We only had an hour and I thought to myself, 'Why bother? An hour'll be over like that.' We were in a car park and he held my hand and he told me stories. Then he was gone. Next time, we only had ten minutes. But I realized that it didn't matter. In those ten minutes, I could learn more, experience more, than in an entire lifetime." She waves an arm at the sky, the sleeve of her fleece jacket fluttering. "This concept we have of time, it's so silly, really. We worry, run around thinking, 'Oh my God, oh my God, I have so little time.' But you see, even just ten minutes can be everything."

"It sounds amazing," I say. "This type of love."

"Dear boy." Her face softens. "You're scared that you might never experience it, but you will. You've got to be vulnerable, that's all."

A sudden flash, Sue on the phone, asking, "Did...you... trust...me?" Her voice tight, almost pleading. The memory makes me wince.

"There's no other way?" I ask.

She purses her lips. "You would prefer something else?"

"I wouldn't mind."

"Listen," she says after a beat, "we must be vulnerable. In life and in love. It's by being vulnerable that we learn. It's our vulnerabilities that move us forward, not our strengths. That's why I so do not like convention. Convention says: be strong. Especially for a man: be strong, don't show emotion. Poppycock! My greatest strength is my vulnerability."

A nearby stream has overflowed and the trail grows wet. We step carefully around puddles and slippery rocks. I offer her my hand for support and she grabs it, smiling.

"What was it about him?" I ask. "What made you love him?"

She stares at our hands. "I can't name it exactly. You know, all my life, others have wanted to know me, but he was the first who said, 'I want you to know everything about me.' And the way he kissed, I could feel all of him in a single kiss." She pauses as we focus on reaching dry ground. Once we can walk freely, she lets go. "And it's not as if he knew everything about me," she says. "He knew a bit of everything about me, and I suppose that was enough." She thinks for a moment, then says, "I used to feel so safe with him. I told him that once, and he asked, 'Why do you feel safe with me?' It was the same feeling as when I left my parents to go live with my grandmother, but I suppose that wasn't the best thing to say to him."

She laughs softly, then doesn't say anything.

"How'd you meet?" I ask.

"At work. I was on set one day, standing next to this handsome man while he talked to the director. I was waiting for the director, we needed to talk about something, I don't quite remember. Gosh, it's all a bit fuzzy now. Anyway, this man, he took my palm in his own and started stroking it gently. All without appearing conscious of what he was doing." She runs a hand through her hair and holds it there. She turns to me. "Can you imagine? There I was, forty-three, mother of four. I had no intention of having an affair." The hand drops. "I'm not a philanderer. I don't go around rooting for men. I've never rooted for a man in my life."

Her staff taps against rocks with each step. I count sixteen taps before she speaks again.

"We talked, and then, we were meeting in a car park once a week. It was innocent, really. I told him about my childhood, about my husband, the large, rambling house that we lived in, and I told him something I hadn't realized before: now that I had what I wanted, I was lacking something. I was always rushing about so, taking care of everyone, but I never had time for myself. I tell you what, he did something brilliant. He listened."

She stops, smiles. Tiny wrinkles below her eyes spread out to her cheeks.

"One of your best qualities, dear boy."

I smile big and wide, happy.

"His wife, she was very beautiful and charming. I remember I used to think, 'Gosh, what is he doing with me?' He told me how she was withdrawn from him. He talked about the women he had been with—and there were many—and how he was secretly afraid of getting close to a woman."

She nudges me gently with her elbow, then continues.

"The first time I went to his house, his wife was away. He made me dinner. I couldn't remember when anyone had done such a simple thing for me. We were in the kitchen and I pointed out a cup I liked, it reminded me of one my grandmother used to have. From then on, whenever I visited him, he always gave me something to drink in that cup.

"When I left, I fell down the stairs. There I was, trying to be calm and composed even though I was giddy inside, and I just went tumbling into the living room."

We both have a good laugh.

"What would this man think? Me acting like a schoolgirl! Well, I got to my feet, pretending like nothing had happened, went out the door, tripped and fell in the garden. Tell you what, I managed to make it to the car without falling again."

She waits until I'm done laughing.

"And I tried, I really did. Any reason to stop, to find something wrong, but I couldn't. There was nothing wrong with this love I felt. It opened me up far more to my patients, and I passed this love to them.

"Then one day, as you can imagine, he asked if I would ever consider leaving my husband. I couldn't bear the thought of hurting my husband. He's such a good man. And I did love him. Next day, I met Julian at the conservatory. I remember he was sitting there, surrounded by these greeny things, and I said to him, 'I can't.'

"He said, 'Well, I guess we shouldn't see each other.'

"He was only sitting a bit away from me. I said to him, 'You feel so far away,' and he said, 'You can come closer.'

"I couldn't. The decision had been made. I walked to my car and lit a cigarette with shaky hands. I looked up and saw this jay—they were quite rare around there—and I thought to myself, 'I have never felt such pain.'

"Three weeks later, I was somewhere near Oxford. It was a beautiful day, birds in the air, a pond nearby, and a three-story house, all crooked. At the top, the window was open and someone was playing the flute. I stood there and listened to that beautiful music. I looked at the pond and realized why some people jump into the nearest body of water to finish it all. The pain. The emotional pain was so intense, so powerful, I didn't know what to do."

The trail has widened into a gravel path. We step aside to let a pilgrim on a bicycle pass. Behind us, fields rustle.

"I didn't call him," Kat says. "I thought I'd never see him again. Six or eight months later, I was in the studio, eating my breakfast, and I saw him. I thought he'd just popped out of my head; I'd just made him up. But he was chatting with some producers. He walked over and gave me the most sensual kiss one can at eight-thirty in the morning.

" 'Will you wait for me?' he asked.

" 'I can't. I've got to go to work.'

"I walked off set, but I was numb all day. I'd pass him, sitting and talking with the directors, and he'd blow kisses at me and wave his arms all about. I thought, 'Gosh, this man's twenty-one years older than me and he's like an adolescent in love.'

"Later that evening, I saw him and he asked what time I was getting off. I told him eight o'clock. 'I can't wait that long,' he said. I walked him to the gates, which weren't very far. I thought that would be safe, otherwise I might get in his car and never return. He kissed me on the neck at the gate and walked away. I watched his back and I called out, 'Are you all right?'

"He said, 'I'm all right. Just.'

"What did he mean, 'All right. Just'?"

"Two or three days later, I was on set and I saw a phone in the corner. It seemed as if it were flashing at me. I'd tried to call him once before but the coin had gotten stuck and I thought to myself, 'Good God, woman, let it go.' Well, now I didn't. I called and heard his voice. His soft, gentle voice. 'You're welcome to come by,' he said, and I did.

"Well, I got lost and was three hours late. He opened the door. There was no 'Oh my God, what took you so long?' He just looked at me and said, 'There you are. I thought you'd disappeared,' and he put his arms around me and held me for the longest time."

The corners of her eyes tighten as she smiles.

"Well," she says. "You can guess what came next."

Wooden fences line the road. We pass horses grazing, farmhouses, cowsheds, and streams with wooden bridges. Suddenly, a cloud shifts and the sun shines through. The wind slows. A large cloud covers the sun and the wind picks up again.

We continue walking. The edges of the clouds are faint reds and yellows, their bottoms a turquoise gray. There are lots of breaks in the clouds now and hundreds of beams shine over the land, some slanted at angles, others pouring straight down.

"Gosh." Kat brings a hand to her chest. "This is so very beautiful."

The road climbs, and far ahead, we see it curve through a meadow and enter the forest.

"How long did you know him?" I ask.

"Eight years."

"Wow," I say, surprised. "Long time."

"Yes. I was terrified of losing him. I told him that. I used to think, 'Please, please, please, oh please, never leave. I don't know how I'll cope. I'll shrivel up and die.' I couldn't bear the thought."

She is quiet. I count twelve taps, wondering what it might be like to feel this way.

"One time," she says, "I didn't see him for a year and I didn't know if I'd ever see him again."

"Why?"

"It was his age, you see, and medical conditions. It became difficult for him to make love, and then he couldn't. When that happened, he held me close and said, 'It just means that I can fully concentrate on giving you pleasure.' But I could see how difficult it was for him to accept it. I asked him, 'What's it like?'

"He said, 'Imagine that I'm standing at the front door. It's open. You are upstairs. You can hear me. I'm calling out to you but you cannot speak. You cannot move to come see me. That is what it's like to not be able to make love to you.'"

A flock of white birds rises through the trees and circles overhead. They ride the wind, growing higher and higher. Kat watches them until they stop circling and fly east.

"It got to be so that it was difficult for him to be near me," she says. "He couldn't bear the pain. Finally, he told me that we should stop seeing each other. We could talk on the phone, but being near was too painful.

"I thought my world was ending. I tried to change his mind, I begged him, but he wouldn't. I thought I would end up in a padded cell. For a year, I went through life with plate glass windows over my eyes; I wasn't alive. Then one day, we were on the phone and I blurted out, 'I need you!'

"He said, 'You do?'

"'Yes, don't you see? I need you.'

"'Well,' he said, 'in that case, what are you doing this evening?'

"We started meeting in a car park facing a pond surrounded by these tall trees. We would get tea from an adjacent shop, and as we stood in line, he would sing to me. Classical songs, old English nursery rhymes. He would hold my hand, look into my eyes, and sing. Then we would sit in the car and talk for hours and laugh, and when he kissed me, it was so sensual. Oh, I felt so beautiful."

We pass cows grazing in pastures, bells around their necks clinking. The grass grows thicker and is soon replaced by ferns

and bushes. Cork oaks and chestnuts border the road as it narrows into a dirt trail, and then we are in the forest.

It's quiet and cool walking under the trees. I don't disturb
her, knowing that she will finish the story in her own time. The
trail is littered with rocks and leaves. We pass fallen trees, their
barks rotting, roots reaching upward.

Dry mud walls grow higher along both sides until we're
walking in a deep, wide trench. Even though the trail winds
uphill, it feels like we are descending. Thick trees lean over
from above, their leafy branches meshing overhead. Soon, the
branches have enveloped the trench like the arcing roof of a
cathedral and the mud walls are up to our heads.

We are in a tunnel with a green roof. We walk until we
can't see the entrance behind us anymore. When the wind
blows, the roof shivers. Light filters through the leaves, and far
ahead, the tunnel narrows into a bright oval.

We sit on a tree stump while Kat lights a cigarette. She
starts to take a puff, but coughs hard instead.

"You okay?" I ask, reaching out to steady her.

"Yes, dear boy. I'm all right. Thinking about him, it brings
emotions, you know." She sucks on the cigarette. In the darkened tunnel, the tip glows like a firefly. "Ah, I do so need this."

She takes another puff and exhales. Like a long sigh.

"I used to tell him that I knew what he was thinking," she
says quietly, "what he was feeling. My emotions were so strong.
I'd try to tell him what I felt but the words wouldn't come. I'd
tell him that words are so hard. He'd take my hand and say,
'Yes, but they are also useful.'"

She chuckles at the memory and smokes until only the

filter remains. Then she flicks it. The filter spirals through the air and bounces off the wall. I glance at the wedding band on her finger and can't help myself.

"Does your family know?"

She looks away. "Hmm...yes."

I don't know why, but I push further. "How'd they find out?"

"My children, well, they learned on their own, really. One day I was going to see Julian and my youngest son asked, 'Where're you off to?' and I made some excuse. I drove away and thought what a horrible thing I'd done. I had never lied to my children before. Never. It's disgraceful to lie to your children. I saw Julian, returned home, and I said to him, 'I've just lied to you for the first time in my life.'"

"Did your husband...did he, I mean, did he—"

"Yes, I told him."

"You did?"

In a tunnel of mud and trees, her voice is hollow. "I always wanted to tell him. I wanted to ask him what to do, hoping he'd say, 'You poor thing, it's just a sickness, you'll pass through,' but of course, I didn't. Not until much later. It had been years by then, you see.

"I waited for him to return from work. I was a wreck. When he came, I was in the dining room and there was a scotch on the table. I said, 'I think you should drink this.' He didn't want it, so I drank it; I needed it. I told him that if at least he wasn't going to drink, then he'd better sit down."

She stops, her face pale. I offer her my bottle and she takes several sips.

"If this is too hard," I say, capping the bottle, "you don't have to."

Eyes piercing, she looks at me. "No. You should know this."

The wind picks up and the branches in the roof shake. Leaves float down from above.

"Sometimes when I look at my husband," she says, "I think, 'Oh, how I've made you suffer.' I just want to honor that remarkable man. When I told him, he said that Julian must be an amazing man for me to love him the way I did."

"He said that?"

She nods. "It wasn't easy, mind you; it was hard. Terribly, terribly hard. He was very angry, but we've worked through it." She shivers and pulls her jacket around her. "We've been so conditioned. We've been brought up to think that there is only one type of love. It's rubbish, really. There's so many types. It took me a long time to realize that I could love my husband and Julian. They were different types of love, really. Both taught me a lot. They just taught me different things."

She is quiet again and chews her lip. I wait, then ask, "Did you ever see Julian again?"

"Oh yes, I continued seeing him. Now that my husband knew, I would tell him when I went to the car park. He knew that there wasn't any, well, you-know-what going on, given Julian's medical condition and all. He trusted me."

"Sounds like quite a guy."

"Yes. Yes, he is. I'm very fortunate." She glances around, searching. "I say, I do need a walk."

She retrieves the cigarette butt and shoves it inside her jacket pocket. We start down the trail.

"Are you okay?" I ask.

She says nothing.

"If this brings up memories, if you'd rather not talk about it," I offer again, "it's okay."

"No." She rubs her eyes with her palms. "It's quite all right. My experience with Julian was perfect, and his death, too, was part of that perfection. But it was difficult to accept in the beginning."

"How did it...?" I start to ask, but stop, noticing her face. The color is gone. Her cheeks are like paper and I can make out thin veins underneath.

"He had cancer."

My mouth suddenly feels acidic. I swallow several times to get rid of the taste.

"One evening, we were in the car park, sipping tea, and he said, 'I have something to tell you,' and I said, 'Yes?' He said, 'I have been diagnosed with cancer.'" A muscle on her jaw quivers. "The cancer had a high survival rate, you see. He just needed to have an operation. But after the operation, his body succumbed to infection. I went to visit him at the hospital every day. I met his wife; she thought I was a friend. He continued losing weight, and one evening, I sensed something about him, the same I had experienced with dying patients. I begged him, pleaded with him to get better. 'Oh, please, please get better; I can't go on without you.' But he slipped into a semi-coma."

She blinks, eyes on the end of the tunnel and the oval of light.

"You know, once, while sitting next to his bed, I turned to a nurse and said, 'This man is so very special to me.' She said, 'I know. We can tell.'

"And his wife, she wanted to be my friend. I had become a source of support for her. It was odd because I was having an affair—oh, how I hate that word, it doesn't even begin to describe what it was—with her husband. I was there for her, I helped her. I remember I used to think, 'I hope that someday she finds what I found with her husband.'"

We pass the white trunk of a beech tree. She reaches over, plucks a leaf, holds it against her nose and inhales deeply.

"Then one day," she says, voice faint, "I stopped pleading. I told him how much I loved him and I would always love him. Then I went home. Soon after, I got the phone call from his wife that he was near death."

We resume walking. She holds the leaf tight in her hand.

"When I reached the hospital, he was in a coma but still alive. His wife was there. We sat by his bedside and I said to her, 'I want you to know that I love your husband.' She said, 'I know.' We sat for hours, then his wife left to get some tea. I was alone with him. I thanked him one more time for the beauty he had brought into my life and I said, 'When you leave, I will go to the car park and think of you. I will be with you.' And he opened his eyes just as I finished speaking. He looked at me. At that moment, his wife walked in, and I left to give them time together."

The branches of the roof have thinned and sunlight patches the trail. Our packs brush against mud walls.

"He died shortly thereafter," she says. "When I saw his body, it looked so beautiful, like it was glowing. I asked his wife if I could kiss him goodbye and she said yes. I bent over and kissed him on the forehead, where I always did when he was alive, and as I did, I could actually feel him—the very essence of who he was, it was so strong—I could hear him saying, 'Oh, you're such a wolly, kissing me just after I've died. You always were a sentimental old bat.'"

The trench walls lower to shoulder level.

"I went to the car park and walked to the shop to get some tea. It was there, I think, when I realized it—standing in line and ordering tea for one instead of two—I nearly collapsed. Afterward, I took the tea and went for a walk amongst the trees, and without any warning, I felt him. The feeling was so strong that I said, 'Back off a bit,' and it did, just as the wind died. Then I realized it was him and I begged him to return, and the wind started again and I felt him."

The mouth of the tunnel is closer, the light brighter. The walls are at our waists.

"Now whenever I walk and feel the wind, I feel him. Not as strongly as that day, but I feel him and it's wonderful."

The walls are down to our knees and the trench widens. The mouth of the tunnel is a bright white.

"His death has given me an understanding into the purity of love. How strong it can be even though that person is no longer there."

The tunnel ends. One moment we were under a roof of branches and leaves, and the next, we're in a meadow. I hear a stream and look around, but can't see it. To our left is a valley, then hills.

We walk through the tall grass, the wind flapping the bottoms of our pants. The trail winds higher. We walk and we walk and we walk. I've never seen her like this. She pushes forward, faster and faster, as if burning something off. My calves hurt. We continue rushing, seeing nothing, until we reach the crest of a hill, and then we stop. We sit on our packs and gaze out over the valley.

"After Julian died," she says quietly, "I looked at my body and thought, 'What's this?'" She gestures at the sky. "For the first time I felt as if my soul was out there. And this...this shell. I felt completely out of my body and realized that death is only a small piece of the whole."

She opens a bag of olives. Seeing it brings back the memory of our first lunch.

"All the fears we have about our bodies," she says, "we worry about getting old, our stomachs growing, wrinkles popping up; none of it matters. This body is nothing but a shell." She rests both arms on her knees, the bag dangling from her fingers. "I just wanted to leave it behind and join him." She lets the bag drop. "Our bodies, they crumble. Death is only a blip, just a blip in...whatever."

Her shoulders rise and fall as she breathes. Her eyes still have that faraway look, but there is something different. It is as if they aren't looking at the distance, but through it.

"Talking about him," she says, "it brings back many memories, even silly ones. He was partially deaf in his left ear, and when we were having a tender moment, I would whisper to him. He would turn to me and shout, 'What?' I would shout back and we would laugh." She looks straight at me, her gaze so strong that I almost flinch. "It's remarkable what you miss when they're gone."

With shaking hands, she lights another cigarette and inhales deeply.

"I've been so blessed," she says. She's smiling now. "I believe that. There's so much beauty in my life, and when I think of it, gosh, it just takes my breath away."

She points at me with the cigarette.

"Remember that, special boy. Never forget the beauty."

The sun has disappeared behind the hills. A thin, red line glows across the crests, as if they are on fire.

"I won't, Kat."

Streaks of clouds drift above. The red on the hills intensifies and the underbellies of the clouds turn a fierce orange.

"Kat, I think this is definitely a cigarette moment."

She hands me a cigarette and lights it. The color is back in her cheeks.

"I do worry about you, you know," she says, watching me inhale.

"Last one," I say, holding the cigarette out.

"Well, I do worry," she says and laughs. "My children complain that I tend to get a bit mummyish."

We smoke in silence. There is only the occasional howl from the wind. The hills fade first, then the clouds. They are mostly gray now, their edges tinged with red. The rest of the sky, a light blue, turns darker. As we finish the cigarettes, the wind grows colder and crickets begin to chirp. According to a sign we passed, the next village is less than a kilometer away.

"Brr," I say, my face tingly. "Want to head on?"

She nods, smiling, and I help her stand.

"After his death," she says, "for a while, nothing mattered. The children were grown up and didn't need me, really. My husband didn't need me—at least that's what I thought, incorrectly—anyway, I didn't want to be here." The wind whips at us with a low whistle. Her smile is still there. "But I'm glad I stuck around."

I look at her: the gentle eyes, the wrinkles, the silver hair, the red cheeks. I have known her for such a little time but now can't imagine my life without her. I reach out, hold her hand. We both smile.

"Me too, Kat," I say. "I'm so glad you stuck around."

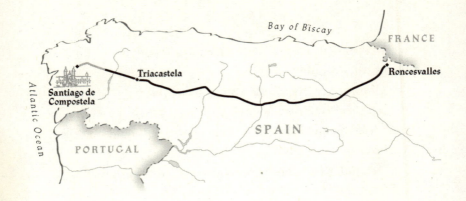

# Day Thirty-six

I walk slowly, leaning on a thick branch for support, one ankle wrapped tight in an elastic bandage, courtesy of a wet floor at a refuge. By midafternoon, I catch up with Kat. She's resting at the edge of a stream, boots off, feet in the water.

"Oh, helloey," she calls out as I near. "I say, how's that foot?"

I drop my pack and sit down. "Getting better."

"Let's take a look," she says.

I remove my boot and sock and unwrap the bandage. She puts her glasses on and examines it gently, pressing the ankle. The way she touches, it barely hurts. I tell her that.

"Well," she murmurs, turning the foot in her hands, "I've had a bit of practice, you know."

I lean back and gaze up at the trees. The sunlight warms my face. The rushing sound of a small waterfall downstream.

"How are the fears?" I hear her say.

I noodle it over. Thanks to the medication she got, the eyes are slowly healing, and when I think of my father and his suffering, I feel sadness, but my stomach doesn't tighten the way it used to.

"Still there," I say, "but not as much. And they're not getting to me."

I feel her rub cream into my ankle.

"It's all right to have fears," she says. "Just recognize them for what they are: not real. Then don't listen to them. That's important."

I sit up on my elbows. "Your fears, they ever come back?"

"They have a rather nasty habit of popping up now and then," she says, capping the tube. "I tell you what, they don't have the same power, and now I know how to focus on reality. They only pop up when I'm under a lot of stress, like you have been lately. So I'm kind and gentle to myself, and they leave. That's what you've got to do: take care of yourself. And they will disappear."

She unrolls a new bandage and wraps my ankle. I lean back again. Somewhere behind me, a cricket sings its lonely song.

"Right." She pats my leg. "There you are."

I stand, test the foot. The bandage is snug and the ankle barely hurts. We hoist our packs and walk along the sandy, white trail to a field.

Normally, I have to slow down when we're together, but now, her pace is just right. A pilgrim had nicknamed the way she walked, "the Kat shuffle." She loved that.

The trail intersects another trail, creating four perpendicular paths. We pause, gaze around. There is only us, the path vanishing into four directions, wheat stalks, wind.

"We could go anywhere," I say. "New places, new adventures."

"Hmm," she says. "That's what makes life so magical. One always has choices."

In the middle of the intersection, three long sticks, painted yellow, are arranged in the shape of an arrow. We follow it, hobbling and shuffling until another yellow arrow guides us into the woods. A slight breeze blows dirt off the trail, and walking under the shade, we are quiet.

The trail twists through the trees. I focus most of my energy trying not to slip on loose rocks. Soon, the trail widens and I get slightly ahead of Kat.

"Hang on a tick," I hear her call out.

I turn to see her standing under a thick oak. A small square sign nailed into the trunk reaches her shoulders. I slowly make my way over.

"This is so very beautiful." Kat brushes a hand over the sign. "What do you suppose it means?"

The top of the wooden sign reads "Exp de Selix." Underneath, a cross enclosed by a half circle, like a bowl. The whole thing in a full circle, all of it red.

"It's pretty," I say, "whatever it is."

"Hmm." She nods, continues staring.

We return to the trail. It curves lazily, and when it straightens, there's Nick, taking photos of a boulder. Painted on it, the same symbol. Below it, a red arrow points down the trail. Same direction as the Camino.

Nick gestures toward it. "You found it all right?"

By now, we've run into each other enough times to have civilized conversations. I've even grown to sort of like him.

"Any idea what it is?" I ask.

He shakes his head. Kat gently brushes the symbol with a hand.

"So beautiful," she whispers.

We follow the trail until it ends at a field enclosed by a barbed-wire fence. A yellow arrow on a post points right. Below it, a red arrow points left.

The last time I hadn't paid attention to a sign, I missed out on Ignacio and his wooden cross.

"I want to see where this goes," I say.

Nick nods. "Right. We'll have a look."

"An adventure." Kat smiles. "I say, this is rather exciting."

For the first time on the Camino, we follow arrows that aren't yellow. They head deep into the woods to a trail that branches several times, twists through oaks, leads past a corn-field, and ends at a two-storied farmhouse.

The white paint on the walls is peeling in long strips. Patches of mud and brown grass make up the lawn. Two small tracks the width of tires lead to the garage.

"All right, then," Nick says, glancing around.

We stand in the heat, sweat drying off our necks. A sparrow starts to chirp. Just as I'm about to prove myself a rude American and go knock on the door, there is a loud creak. The garage door opens and a man in a blue jumpsuit runs out.

By the time he reaches us, he is panting. His graying hair is neatly trimmed, there is slight stubble on his face, and he has sharp blue eyes. The zipper on the jumpsuit is open to his chest, showing a white T-shirt underneath. He rests his hands on his knees and catches his breath.

"My," Kat says, hand on her chest. A big smile.

"I am very happy to see you," the man says in Spanish, then adds something I can't understand. Each region in Spain has its own dialect, and the one here in Galicia confuses even native speakers of Spanish.

"Come." He gestures for us to follow.

While Nick and I give each other that "should we?" look, Kat and the man are already on their way to the garage.

He pauses and waves. "Please."

By the time we're inside, Kat's pack is on the dirt floor and she's already on her first cigarette. Bales of hay are stacked against the back wall. On the far end is a wire fence, and behind it, in the darkness, chickens cluck.

The man wipes his face with his sleeve. Kat smokes and watches him quietly. A sheep bleats.

"What do we do?" Nick nudges me and whispers.

"Beats me," I whisper back.

The man flicks a switch on the wall. Sharp red and blue light shoots out of a doorway and lights up the dirt floor.

"Come." He motions. "Come."

While we remove our packs, Kat is already through the doorway. Hollow footsteps on wooden stairs.

"Good Lord." Kat's voice, loud.

I drop the branch and run after her, Nick behind me. There are stories of people getting attacked on the Camino. We bound up stairs lit with Christmas lights to the long rectangular room. She's standing beside the man.

"You all right?"

"Of course, dear boy," she says. "This is brilliant."

Paintings line the walls. Feeling more than a little foolish, I calmly go to the nearest painting, as if I storm up stairs every day. Kat's boots echo on the hardwood floor as she walks back and forth, murmuring, "Oh my, goodness gracious, oh my."

The painting is large, with two trees, their trunks resembling palms cupped together in prayer. Behind the trees, a large circle of orange and green spirals into itself. The sky, through the branches, glitters white.

Hands in his jumpsuit pockets, the man watches us. All the paintings are like this. Trees, sky, birds, all glittering. He walks over to Kat and says something.

"Oh, really?" she says. "Yes, of course."

The color, there's something different about it. It's not paint, more like fine, shimmering grains of sand. Even the canvases are covered with it. The man follows me to a painting of yellow hills under a reddish sky.

"Stone." He rubs a fist into his palm, a grinding motion.

I shake my head, not understanding. He pulls a dark green crystal the size of a golf ball out of his pocket, places it in my hand, then points to the adjoining room. Thin beams of light shine through shuttered windows to a table covered with rocks, crystals, and paintbrushes. Beside it, a bookshelf lined with glass pickle jars, each shimmering with color. Turquoise blue, reddish brown, sparkling green, orange the color of a sunset.

"No paint," the man says. "Everything comes from stone."

"Where do you find your stones?" Kat asks.

"I walk with a bag. Like you. Sometimes I dig."

"But the detail," Kat blurts out in English. "It must take forever."

The man nods, seeming to understand.

"Yes. It depends on the size. That"—he points to a painting with three trees—"it took four months. But this is what I love."

While he opens the windows, we study the paintings. Outside, the sky is a light afternoon blue. I join Kat. She has her glasses on and is staring at the painting of the two bare trees with the spiral.

"It's very beautiful," she says to me. "It reminds me of lovers growing into each other through eternity."

The man walks over and I ask him what the painting means.

"Mystery," he says. "The mystery of life."

"And love," Kat adds.

He turns to her, practically memorizing her face, then smiles. "Yes. Love and life, a beautiful mystery."

As I walk away, she asks how he comes up with the designs. He replies slowly but I only catch three words: Heart. Dream. Stone.

"Come," the man says after a while. "Tea?"

"Oh, that would be lovely," Kat says.

I don't want to leave just yet.

"Can I?" I point at the paintings.

The man nods yes.

While Kat and Nick follow him downstairs, I hold the crystal in my hand, the sharp edges on my palm, and try to imagine the sheer force of rock against rock and the thousands of centuries it might have taken to produce it. I remember feeling that way about the Himalayas in India. I'd trekked in those mountains, watched the sun rise and set over the peaks, and all that time I had been trying to escape the past. But it was the upheaval of the past, the violence of tectonic plates crashing against each other, that had created the mountains.

I wander around, gaze out the window at an old oak,

its trunk straight and narrow like a redwood, the branches spreading out wide. Then, me being me, I have to peek inside his studio. And there it is leaning against the wall, larger than all the others: wings outstretched, golden and fiery, rising from the earth to the sky, ablaze. Every single grain shimmers.

I walk over and stare at it for a long time. Nothing surprises me on this walk anymore.

"I'm glad you're no longer at bottom," I whisper.

Her voice, far away. "I'm glad you're not there either."

"The view up here's much better, isn't it?"

I feel her smile. This moment, so much crammed into it. Her, India, my father, this crazy walk. And the one thread is the immense gratitude I feel for it all. Every single step that led me to this, and from here, the steps to come.

"If it made you who you are," Loïc once said, "then it is good."

I get it now. I actually get it.

I throw the crystal in the air, watch it reflect the light, glitter, and catch it. I grin, then remember that we still have a long day's walk ahead. Returning the crystal to the table, I take a final look at the painting.

They are at the kitchen table downstairs, smoking. The man leads us back to the garage.

"Wait," he says, dragging a small mortar and pestle to our packs.

He scrounges around the dirt floor and finds an ordinary-looking rock. He chips at it with a hammer and a chisel until several pieces fall off, then holds it up like a trophy. A vein of green shines in the middle.

"Good lord," Kat says, her voice hushed.

He extracts the green with the chisel and grinds it in the mortar. When he's done, there are tiny, sandlike particles inside, just like the ones in his paintings. They glitter. He carefully hands the mortar to Kat.

She rubs a finger along the inside edge, turning it green.

"How did you know?"

"The stone guides me."

Finally, we shoulder our packs and walk to the lawn. He tells us about a shortcut to the Camino, shakes our hands, looking into Kat's eyes for a long time, and walks back to the garage.

The trail leads past the field and into the woods. While Nick takes the lead, Kat and I walk behind slowly, leaning on our staffs.

"I'm so glad we followed the red arrow," I say to her.

"So am I," she says. "He was a simple and wise man. He was telling me about the symbol we saw on the sign. He made it out of love for a woman. It depicts love, the soul, sexuality, and eternity. It finishes in a circle to show how we are complete in the scheme of life and death. Isn't it brilliant?"

I nod. We stop to drink from our bottles.

She stares ahead, her voice soft. "I've got a feeling that wisdom has nothing to do with knowledge, but having a sense of wonder. The older I get, the more I realize that we really can't answer many of life's questions. It is a mystery and a beautiful one at that. I've learned to accept it."

We resume and reach the fields. Yellow arrows lead us along the fence and then to a gravel road lined with poplars. There is no breeze, only heat and silence, and it feels good to walk under the shade.

"I tell you what," she says. "He was so passionate, but what he said was simple. He said, 'I work in stone, and in my stone, I find everything. I find God, the world, myself.'"

She turns to me, smiles.

"Dear boy, we all need to find our stone."

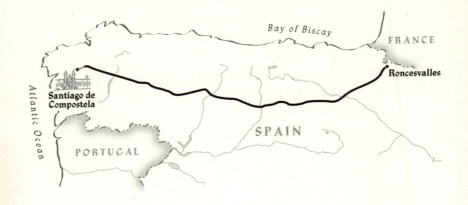

## Day Thirty-seven (Morning)

I find a phone booth across the street from a café and dial her number. When she picks up, I say playfully, "Hi, Sue, remember me?"

"Mister pilgrimage himself?"

I laugh. She waits a beat, then joins.

"Still with what's-his-name?"

A pause, then, "Yes."

"It's okay," I say. "That's not why I called anyway. I called... I just called... because..."

"Yes?"

"I'm glad you're doing well." I stare through the glass at the hills. "As for me, I'm all right. I wanted you... I needed you to know that."

"Oh," she says, her voice tender, then she is quiet for a long moment. "Oh, Amit."

"And I'd like to see you."

"You're coming back?"

"I have to send out med school applications."

"That's great," she says. "I always thought you should."

I want to treat patients with love, like Kat. I'm tempted to tell Sue about her, but let it go. How does one possibly explain Kat in all her Katness anyway?

"I know," I say. "I want to give the world what it needs: another Indian doctor."

She laughs, fully this time. Such a magical sound.

"I want us to be friends," I continue. "I want to come back and tell you everything."

"I'd like that," she says. "I'd like that a lot."

"And I'm glad you're with him."

"Listen—"

"You deserve someone who makes you happy. I wasn't that guy."

The line buzzes, quiet. "You too, Amit."

We both soak in the moment.

"I'm believing it more and more," I finally say.

After we finish, I cross the street to the café, and join Kat at our table. Tomorrow, we will be at the cathedral in Santiago. In the phone booth, I saw something that gave me an idea.

"I'm going to camp there tonight," I say to her, pointing at the hills.

She cups a hand over her eyes, peers up. Once you notice it through the trees, it's unmistakable.

"Bloody good idea."

She grins, rubbing my hair fondly. It reminds me of my aunt. That feels like forever ago. I must call her in Santiago and thank her for putting up with me.

"I'll catch up with you tomorrow before the cathedral."

"Of course you will, dear boy," Kat says. "I will just be plodding along."

After she leaves, I order a *café con leche*, and drink it slowly, occasionally dipping bread into the milky coffee. After tomorrow, I will wake up without anywhere to walk to. The thought makes me a little sad, because this has been my life for the past thirty-six days, but it makes me smile too, because with the end of one journey will come another. That's what life is anyway: new journeys.

I gaze out to where the street curves through the village. A yellow arrow on the sidewalk points to the hills. Could my father have seen this when he asked me to take his ashes to the Ganges? Me preparing to finish a Catholic pilgrimage? Definitely not. Did he know that going to India would set off a journey where I would finally be able to give him what I couldn't when he was alive: forgiveness? Maybe. Who knows the mind of a dying man? But this I know: although the threads of his DNA are embedded in mine, I am not him. He was a product of his experiences, and I, a product of mine.

Perhaps violence was an invisible thread, linking generations, from his grandfather to his father to him. But the choice of continuing it, of carrying it on to further generations, is mine. My choice. And I choose for it to end.

Realizing that lets me feel closer to him. I see him as a child, playing with his sister, a father who made mistakes, and now, whenever I think of him, I feel fondness for the man, and sadness for what was and what could have been.

Somewhere in the village, church bells ring. A pigeon lands

on the sidewalk and struts back and forth on red claws. It watches me sideways with a round, open eye, then flies away.

I leave money for the coffee on the table, slide the chair back, and stand. My pack is at my feet. I hoist it, feel the familiar weight settle on my shoulders, tighten the straps, and clip on the waist belt.

Then I take a deep breath and head toward the hills.

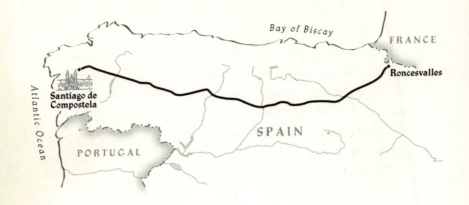

# Day Thirty-seven (Afternoon)

I snap the branch against my thigh, break it in two, and throw it on the pile. I look past the stone fortifications to where the hillside slopes downward, dark and jagged with pines, then smooths out into a meadow. The trees sway slightly in the wind. Far below, a reservoir shimmers. Beyond it is a road and then the village from where I first saw the ruins of this castle. And now, a half hour's climb later, I'm here.

I jump down from the outer wall, about a five-foot drop, and gather the pile in my arms. Inside, the castle is mostly uneven ground with patches of brown grass. I drop the wood near the low pit. There is enough for a small fire.

I arrange rocks around the pit in a circle. The small branches go in first, leaning against each other, and between them, crumpled newspaper. Medium-sized branches go on top. Finished, the whole resembles an inverted cone. The largest branches get stacked on the side for later.

A cloud moves and the sudden sunlight feels good on my face. It's late afternoon and already, my nose is tingly from the cold. I gather more branches for the pile, then explore, but find nothing of interest. Portions of the castle's front wall have crumbled and beer bottles are strewn around the blackened stains of previous fires. The whole thing isn't much larger than a suburban house. Still, I am in a castle, and it's all mine.

In a few hours, the sun will dip behind the hills. If Kat were here, this would be a cigarette moment. But no more of those. Two villages ago, she chucked her remaining cigarette carton into a garbage can.

"Fears or habits or rocks," she said. "We leave something behind."

The faint spires of the Cathedral of Santiago de Compostela are in the distance, and I will be there tomorrow, pressing my fingers into the famous statue, just another pilgrim. I think of the people I met on this walk, the things we talked about, the lessons shared, the hellos and goodbyes. Thoughts and memories come and go. The wind shifts, the trees rustle, and I smile. *Saudade.*

This castle was once home to nobles who sent their henchmen to rob and attack pilgrims. But now, it's in ruins. Someday the forest will reclaim it and nothing will be left. Only the stars will witness the change. I, like the pilgrims before me, will be long gone.

I rub my nose, unable to feel it anymore. Time to work. First: light the crumpled newspaper. It burns quickly, curling inward, edges black. Second: stuff in more paper. Slowly, flames flicker up and down branches. Third: add larger branches. The wood crackles. And fourth, I have it: my very own bonfire in my very own castle. I do a little king-of-the-jungle dance.

When the fire's really going, I lay the thickest branches on top, then crouch and enjoy the moment. Roseangela must be in Santiago by now. I'll find her, ask for a dance. What happens after, no idea. That's the magic of life anyway; one never knows the adventure around the corner.

Soon, my cheeks sting and I shift back slightly. I open a bottle of wine, more for the ritual than anything. One swig, then I slowly pour the rest into the fire.

The night slides in, moonless and crisp with stars. I sit cross-legged, watching the wind whip the flames around. The monk returns.

"That Mara," I say to him, "sure is tricky."

Our smiles grow and I realize just how much they match. He starts to fade.

"Yes." I nod, then whisper. "Yes."

Pieces of ash fly upward, glowing like fireflies. They spiral, float, specks of gold against the sky.

# Acknowledgments

To Stephen and Julia Hanselman at LevelFiveMedia, my amazing agenting team. For your vision and support. Thank you. I love you both.

To Mauro DiPreta at Hachette Books. I remember our first meeting, when I asked who'd be editing this novel, and you said that it was you. I remember how my heart felt at that moment. And it still does. Thank you, my friend.

To the team at Hachette Books. After our first meeting, I walked away impressed. You're all so talented. And you were excited to work with me. How that feels as an author, well, it's the best feeling in the world. A deep thank you to Michelle Aielli, Betsy Hulsebosch, Mark Harrington, Christine Djelevic, Jennifer Kowalski, Melanie Gold, Kara Thornton, David Lamb, Odette Fleming, Roland Ottewell, and all those at Hachette Books who made this dream come true.